Jaye told himself to be patient, to wait.

He just needed to bide his time and wait for his opportunity.

There has to be one. There has to. It can't end like this.

Burt reached behind his back and pulled something out of his belt.

He held it up for Jaye to see and grinned.

Jaye shrieked with all of the air in his lungs, starting to sob, to plead shamelessly, still twisting on those poking, burrowing fingers, the asphalt scraping away more of the skin of his bare butt cheeks.

In Burt's hand was a huge knife, nearly a foot long, but narrow. It was a filleting knife, the kind fishermen used to slice their catch in half or remove its bones.

Also recommended...

You may also enjoy these other ForbiddenFiction works:

Arctic Absolution by Lynn Kelling

In the frozen expanses of remote Alaska, Dixon Rowe is a good man and a good cop who keeps finding himself in bed with the enemy. After he picks up a young ex-con named Jaye Larson for stealing food, Dixon gets seduced by the possibility of helping someone truly in need. Though he tells himself he's assisting young Jaye out of the goodness of his heart, not because of how sexy Jaye is under all of the tattoos and defiance, the temptations of sin entangle them as their hostile environment threatens. Both of their pasts are filled with malicious ghosts that haunt every step, and while Jaye's demons are less tangible than Dixon's, they are all powerful enough to put both of their lives in danger. (M/M)
http://forbiddenfiction.com/story/LK1-1-000188

The Brig by Mason Powell

This classic gay BDSM novel, set near the end of the Viet Nam war, has been out of print for almost 20 years. *The Brig* is a brutally dark erotic drama of a young sailor confined to a military prison where he tortured with pain, fear, sexuality, and mind games to force changes in his psyche and break his spirit. The sailor learns things about himself and his captors that will transform him and challenge those who hold him. (M/M)
http://forbiddenfiction.com/story/mp1-1-000147

Caged Jaye

a prequel to Arctic Absolution

Lynn Kelling

ForbiddenFiction
www.forbiddenfiction.com

an imprint of

Fantastic Fiction Publishing
www.fantasticfictionpublishing.com

CAGED JAYE
A Forbidden Fiction book

Fantastic Fiction Publishing
Hayward, California

© Lynn Kelling, 2016

CREDITS
Editor: Rylan Hunter and D.M. Atkins
Cover Design: Siolnatine
Cover Art: Natalya Nesterova
Production Editor: Erika L Firanc
Proofreading: JhP323

SKU: LK1-000251-02
ISBN: 978-1-62234-285-3

Published in the United States of America

DISCLAIMER

This book is a work of fiction which contains explicit erotic content; it is intended for mature readers. Do not read this if it's not legal for you.

All the characters, locations and events herein are fictional. While elements of existing locations or historical characters or events may be used fictitiously, any resemblance to actual people, places or events is coincidental.

This story depicts fictional BDSM; it is not intended to be used as an instruction manual. It contains descriptions of erotic acts that may be immoral, illegal, or unsafe. The characters are not models for the Safe, Sane and Consensual forms embraced by most current practitioners of BDSM. The author takes license with the use of BDSM for dramatic effect. Do not take the events in this story as proof of the plausibility or safety of any particular practice.

For PJ.
When the world turned upside down,
you kept me steady.
Love you.

Contents

Chapter 1
The End of Normal

Jaye Larson knew he was going to have an awesome birthday, even if he needed to do the work himself to make it happen. He was turning nineteen, inching a little further into the world of responsible adults. There was a lot to feel thankful for. He had a good job, for which he'd worked really hard, and a place of his own with his handsome boyfriend, Kris Garrity. The apartment was located within walking distance to where Jaye's mom lived, which meant he could check in on her as often as he liked. Best of all, on top of all of that, Jaye had all the freedom he could want. If the people closest to him happened to be too bogged down with their own troubles to be able to pitch in with the celebration planning, it only meant it was that much more important for Jaye to show them how much they meant to him.

For three years, he'd been working almost daily at Rick & Pine, a men's designer clothing store. It was one of the best stores in the area to work for, due to their pay scale and reputation for rewarding loyal, hardworking employees. After scouting out a position there since he was only thirteen and too young to apply, Jaye had finally scored the job and wasn't letting it go unless something even better crossed his path. Nothing was more important than earning enough to be independent and making the most of each opportunity that came his way. His mom had always told him he could do whatever he dreamed if he was willing to try his hardest and use his head to carefully think things through. He didn't just believe it was true—he knew it.

Eager to be out and about and get the party started, he wasn't surprised that the day dragged on, tripping over each tick of the clock's minute hand. But, at last, his shift was finally down to the last

1

five minutes. Watching the view of the passing shoppers in the plaza beyond the store's large glass display windows, filled with buff, headless mannequins and large black and white photos of gorgeous, overly styled male models; Jaye felt the wide world beyond calling to him to escape.

The plan was to take off from the store when his shift was done at five o'clock and not a minute after, before anyone could trap him with questions or problems. The evening was too precious to waste. He'd walk the fifteen blocks or so to his mom's place, then meet up with his Kris for dinner. That way, he'd get to spend precious parts of his birthday with the two people who meant more to him than anyone else in the world. Cozy quiet time, some love, and some laughs were all he wanted for gifts. It was all planned out, and nothing was going to go wrong.

He was so excited; he couldn't stop smiling, even when his cheeks started to hurt.

Beaming and practically bouncing with joy, he slipped his customer's merchandise into a Rick & Pine paper tote bag with more male models splashed across each of the panels, then passed it over the check-out counter. The bag contained one pair of carefully refolded, dark-wash, pre-ripped designer jeans.

"Okay, that'll be fifty nine ninety nine, unless... are you signed up for our email newsletter?"

"Nah."

"Well, just this once I could give you the same discount. It's fifteen percent off. Just don't tell anyone I did you the favor." Jaye winked.

"Oh, sweet! Thanks, man."

"No problem." He completed the transaction. The customer looked even happier now and smiled back at Jaye, giving him a little thrill in the process. "Thanks for shopping with us. Have a great night!" Sure, maybe he glanced downward, doing a visual scan of the shape of the guy's shoulders, back, and ass as he turned to go. "Come back soon!" Jaye called after him, probably too eagerly. "Enjoy the jeans!"

Layla snorted with giggles over by the rack of men's button-down shirts where she was restocking some barren shelves.

The shop's door swung shut.

"Okay, Smiley," she teased. "You always flirt way more with the guys." Jaye's customer, wearing some spectacularly form-fitting pants, headed off in the direction of the coffee shop across the shopping center. "Specifically the cute ones."

"Come on. Can you blame me?" Jaye tucked his long, curly, chocolate brown hair back over both ears and tossed the rest over his shoulders so it didn't hang in front of him and block his view. He'd been growing it out since his age was in single digits, with only some trimming of the ends once in a while, so it reached all the way to his lower back. The dark color contrasted with the lightness of his green eyes, which were so pale, they hardly had any color at all inside the darker ring around his irises.

His looks came mostly from his mom, Cora Mitchell, even down to his slender frame and average height. Though Cora had been young when she'd conceived Jaye, she had one of those faces where she looked many years younger than she actually was. No one ever believed they were mother and son, even though Jaye also looked years younger than his age.

He closed up his register and walked over to Layla, who was all blue eyes and dimples, her striped hair a few shades of blonde, dark brown and red all tossed together. At the same time, he tried to keep sight of the hot redhead who'd just left. "Did you see his ass? Total bubble butt. Those jeans looked painted on."

"Sorry, guess my man-ass radar's on the fritz today." Layla glanced back into the recesses of the store where their co-worker Mark had been helping a woman and her teenage son with the fitting room. Layla's smile faltered. Wondering why, Jaye followed her gaze. Mark shot him a pissed off sneer laced with noticeable disgust. Jaye returned the look with a level stare, since he wasn't one to be cowed by narrow-minded douchebags.

"Don't pay any attention to—" Layla started to say.

"The pathetic homophobe? He can kiss my queer ass," Jaye cut in. "I'm the goddamned manager, aren't I? He says a single bigoted word, I'll fire him." He didn't say it loudly, but he didn't whisper it either, which only seemed to make Layla more nervous, shifting from foot to foot.

When Jaye checked over his shoulder again, Mark looked like he was ready to spit on Jaye or pound the cocky grin off of his face. Mark had never followed through on all of the hate, since Jaye did have seniority, if not the height or size advantage. Working at the store for so many years after school, on weekends, and summer holidays got you pretty far if you stuck it out and weren't afraid to put in some effort. He'd been promoted a while ago, and was glad for it. Unlike the rest of Rick & Pine's employees, who were there to socialize and pad resumes, he had no choice but to earn a living. At least it gave him leverage over dicks like Mark.

Layla veered the conversation sideways, sounding like she was trying to distract Jaye from the negative vibes coming from Mark. "But with all the flirting... what about Kris?" she asked. "You two are still good, right?"

In answer, Jaye just gave Layla a wicked little grin, "Oh, come on. It's my job to talk to the customers. So what if I'm a little more talkative with the hot ones?" He nodded in the direction where the customer with the fire-crotch and bubble-butt—one of the best combinations in the world, in Jaye's humble opinion—had disappeared. "Besides, he wasn't even gay. Doesn't count."

"How do you know?"

"Oh, we know," Jaye said heavily, making Layla laugh.

"Gaydar. Right," she agreed. After a pause, giving Jaye a curious little peek, she asked, "So, what are the big birthday plans later?"

"Oh, it's going to be great," Jaye said eagerly. "My birthdays are always a big deal to my mom, so I'm going to stop by her place right after I leave here. I didn't tell her I was coming by, so it'll be a surprise. It'll be great. I've really been missing her. And then it's out for a dinner date with Kris."

"Something super romantic?"

"Of course. Can't wait to get my hands on him. He works so hard, you know? And it's been really rough on him being this far away from his family. He needs the night out just as much as I do," Jaye grinned.

"So, everything's good with you two?"

"Yeah," Jaye scoffed. "It's great. Couldn't be better."

It was a pretty long walk from the store to Cora's apartment and, by the end of it, Jaye could feel blisters forming on his feet, tucked inside nice but hard-soled work shoes rather than padded sneakers. He'd lived in Anchorage, Alaska, his whole life, but never quite got used to the bite of the cold weather. Most of the places he usually needed to go were in walkable distances, but the time constraints of that particular night were hurrying him along. Stuffing his hands deeper into his pockets and burying his mouth in the neck of his coat, Jaye hurried along a little faster to get his blood pumping.

Often, he was able to work out trades with some people who lived in his neighborhood to get rides to places he needed to go. He'd track down the people with vehicles, figure out what they needed or lacked, and helped them get it in order to get an occasional lift. There was a woman on the first floor of his building who worked at the same shopping center he did, so he'd take her dog for walks when she had long shifts and he was home.. Then, she'd let him drive in with her whenever it worked out with their schedules.

Likewise with some of the women his mom danced with. They liked having a guy there with them when going to or from a shift at the club, just for security's sake. Sure, it meant going out of his way or staying up until the wee hours of the morning sometimes, but they always repaid the favor.

But something in the universe just wasn't aligning that particular day. None of his usual contacts had been free that evening to get him back and forth from work, to his mom's, then to his date. So, he tried to tell himself the hike was good exercise.

His mom lived in the same tiny, crappy place he'd moved out of about a year ago. For a long time, he'd been trying to get her to move to a nicer apartment. In his spare time, he'd find the best listings he could for her on the library's computers, then print out all the information and give it to her to look through, circling the features he thought would most draw her interest and making little comments on the margins to cheer her on. It hadn't done any good. The pages would be left on her kitchen counter where he set them, untouched. It was a little frustrating, but he just tried to put himself in her shoes. She didn't want a big rent commitment, and that was understandable. She also had a comfort level and memories invested in her current place.

So Jaye had decided maybe he was better off living with his boy-friend and establishing his own life. That way Cora would be free to get a one-bedroom unit in a better neighborhood instead, save some more money and make a fresh start somewhere new. He also hoped that she would come to visit him often. Maybe seeing how happy he was in a new place would give her more incentive to move on. Sure, the visits didn't happen nearly as often as he'd wished, but there was no rush. She had her own reasons for not wanting to follow through and go just yet. Jaye tried to stay supportive and keep encouraging her.

So far, he was more or less getting along okay. Money was tight but he made enough to scrape by — paying his half of the bills he split with Kris. He couldn't afford a car, let alone the gas and insurance for it. Most of his clothes were designer, but only because of his hefty employee discount at Rick & Pine, his ability to get first crack at any clearance sales, and the stipulation that employees needed to wear the store's clothes while on shift. The furniture and decorations in his apartment were pretty nice, but only because a lot of them had been procured through similar deals with people he knew, or from people he saw getting ready to move, or by watching the curb before trash was collected for unexpected treasures. Some pieces were so nice, Kris had once accused him — lightheartedly — of stealing. But if there was one thing Jaye intended to avoid, it was getting in trouble in any sig-nificant way that would hinder his ability to live the life he wanted to have. It was the same reason he was glad he was a guy and a gay one at that — he'd never make the same mistake his mom did by get-ting saddled with a kid when she was still one herself. Jaye didn't want anything pulling him down, but only sought out platforms from which to launch himself higher.

There wasn't a whole lot of thought for what his future might hold. Jaye knew he couldn't live forever on a retail job's salary, but so far he was making out all right. Jaye believed with all of his heart that everything would keep slowly improving, even if things weren't al-ways picture-perfect with Kris. Jaye knew, from firsthand experience, he could be a hell of a lot worse off than he was. The people around him were always going to be so much more important than the partic-ulars of his circumstances.

Using the key he still had from when Cora's place was still home, Jaye let himself into the apartment on the second floor. Her rundown building was located off a narrow road that was little more than an alley.

"Mom? You here?"

No answer.

His key stuck, so he yanked at it to get it out of the lock, prying it with his foot planted against the door for leverage. It came free and the door ricocheted off the wall with a low bang.

There was no reply.

"Cora! Hey, Cora!"

The place stunk of sour smoke, stale garbage, and rotten food. The curtains were all drawn and no lights were on, so it was hard to make anything out.

"Cora?"

He eyed the overflowing trash can in the kitchen, as well as a few plates of left-out food swarming with flies, maggots and a few shades of healthy mold. Instead of cleaning it up right away, like his sense of smell made him want to, his concern told him to look for his mom first. Her purse was on the hook by the door. It was the most reliable sign, usually, that she was around.

Jaye took a few more steps into the apartment, toward the dingy living room past the narrow, rancid galley kitchen.

He saw her almost right away.

"Shit," he sighed, running a hand over his mouth. Instinct made him hesitate, delaying the inevitable as his birthday fantasies started to blacken and rot. He wasn't going to be getting the warm, loving welcome he'd been hoping for, but that didn't mean he could let Cora down now, especially for selfish reasons.

Grabbing the blanket from the back of the couch, he pulled it free and draped it over Cora. She was lying face-down, sprawled on the couch with her left leg hanging off the side. She was only wearing a pair of sheer light blue panties and a camisole that had slipped off her shoulders. Her kit was open on the coffee table, all laid out. A mostly empty vial stuffed with some white rocks at the bottom rested next to a glass pipe, along with Cora's favorite Hello Kitty lighter.

After she was covered, Jaye felt for a pulse and watched for her breathing. Crouching down by her head, he rested a hand on her bare shoulder and called, gently, "Hey, Mom? You hear me?"

Her light green eyes, dulled by the dark circles surrounding them, were half opened and unblinking. Her cheeks were too hollow, her body way too thin and spotted with random bruises.

When she didn't stir, didn't speak, a memory came back of a birthday ten years earlier, when he was nine. His mom had been so beautiful that day, glowing and laughing, wearing her favorite purple dress — the one with the flowers on the edge of the skirt.

"Wanna know why I decided to name you my Bluejay?" she had asked conspiratorially, sitting with him on the edge of his bed in his little room, barely bigger than a closet, decorated with blue and green dinosaurs on the wallpaper.

"Why?" he asked with a huge smile, completely adoring the hell out of her.

She had kissed his forehead, right in the center of it, and said, "Because, little Jaye, you're gonna fly right out of here someday, to somewhere real pretty. You'll have the whole world and you'll be free."

"You're coming with me, right? When I fly?"

There had been a bruise on her arm, from where a customer had gotten too touchy-feely with her after she'd given them a lap dance. The fingerprints were almost perfectly outlined on her pale skin, but she'd done a good job covering them with makeup. He could hardly see them at all.

She'd smiled at him, looking like an angel with her dark, curly hair spilling over her shoulders. For a minute, she didn't say anything, as though she hadn't heard the question, but just kept on smiling at him like that. When she'd snapped out of it and looked away, she gave his hand a gentle squeeze.

"Course I am, baby," she'd replied. Even at nine years old, he could hear it was a lie. That's why the memory was so vivid. It was one of the ones he replayed, over and over in his head, wondering if she'd already given up, way back then; if her hope had already run out.

He got his bluejay tattoo when he turned eighteen, a few days after his birthday. He'd gotten it for Cora, even though she hadn't been there to see it, or hold his hand while they were inking it painfully into his neck, chest, and back. But, he'd also gotten it to remind him to fly. Leaving that place, that apartment, and *her,* had been his first attempt.

It wouldn't be his last. He'd just wanted to show her it was possible, that he was brave enough to try, and she could be brave too.

Jaye smoothed the dark hair out of his mom's face and kissed her on the forehead like she used to kiss him.

"I'm going out to dinner with Kris. It's my birthday. I'm nineteen," he told her, searching her eyes, hoping to see a reaction or response, even just a faint, little one. The foolish yearning was there in him, telling him to look around the place to see if she'd remembered and left a card or a note wishing him a happy birthday. Afraid of being disappointed, preferring instead to have faith in her, he fought the urge. He wished there was a way to pull her back from wherever those fucking drugs had taken her. He could flush the rest of her shit, but that would only piss her off and make her panic. He didn't know where she hid all her stashes, so it was no guarantee it would even delay her next hit.

She groaned but didn't blink. At least, wherever she was, there were no johns, no people pawing at her, slapping her ass or yelling crude shit. It was the only way she could get out. The only one she knew would work.

"I'm flying, Ma," he said softly, feeling so fucking angry, wanting to smash her pipes, to shake her, to do *something*. He loved her too much to dare. "I'll make a wish for you, okay? When I blow out my candles? I'll use my wish for you."

More of his shiny dream of one really good day withered. There was nothing he could do to stop it. The anger was too close, too big.

He didn't toss her kit.

He just cleaned up the kitchen—tossing the garbage, washing the dishes and wiping the counters down. There were three bags of trash to carry down to the dumpster by the time he was done. Before heading out, he left her a note on the countertop saying he'd been there to check on her, that he loved her and to give him a call when she could, no matter what time it was. Then, he left. If he didn't hurry, he'd be late for meeting up with Kris. The last thing he wanted was to ruin the one good part of his birthday he had to look forward to.

Jogging a little to make up some time, he threw the bags away in the dumpsters behind the building, then just kept jogging, hurrying out to the main road and away, as fast as his sore feet could carry him.

Chapter 2
Birthday with the Boyfriend

Kris wrinkled his nose. The ends of his short, light brown hair were tossed by the wind. He hunched down a little into his black, woolen coat to muffle his mouth and the end of his nose. "You smell like trash."

"Sorry," Jaye apologized, quickly brushing off his coat and pants like that could help. "Something came up and I had to take care of it."

He tried not to involve Kris in his concerns for his mom, preferring instead to bear the burden himself. It was understandable that Kris didn't get it, why it was Jaye's responsibility to fight so hard to get his mom to a better place, mentally, physically and practically. Cora had sacrificed so much for him. It was the least he could do to try and give back as much support as she needed. Plus, Jaye wasn't scared of anything. He could be brave enough for both of them. And the bonus was that it left Kris with more energy to take care of himself.

Jaye tucked his long hair over his left ear, leaning in to kiss Kris's cheek, but Kris pulled away before he could, like he was so offended by the stink, he didn't want Jaye to get closer.

"Sorry. Should I go home and change first?" Jaye offered. They were standing right next to the diner where they were going to eat. Home would be another two mile hike he wasn't sure the blisters on his feet could tolerate.

Checking his watch with a sigh, Kris said, "No. It's already late. Let's just go in."

A waitress seated them at a table near the door. Occasional gusts from outside kept them shivering, but the collective body heat of the patrons inside was sure to help keep them warm. The diner was

11

packed. Almost all the red-vinyl-topped stools were taken and most of the tables, too. The food there had always been reliably great considering how cheap everything was. It was one of Jaye's favorite spots, which was why he'd chosen it for his birthday date with Kris. The slices of cake on the menu were a bonus his raging sweet tooth appreciated. They were always huge portions of a slew of many tempting flavors with heaping mounds of icing, though his favorite was the pistachio cake with honey vanilla buttercream icing. His mouth watered, thinking about it. Just being there, across from Kris, and with nothing left to worry about, made his spirits rise. Slowly, he allowed himself to forget the rest of the things trying to weigh him down.

"This is perfect. I've been looking forward to being here with you all day. Work was good?" he asked Kris, who looked kind of great, actually, in a blue V-neck sweater and khakis. Kris worked in the mortgage department of a local bank, after rising through the ranks from an entry level position he'd landed thanks to a temp agency.

"Yeah, same as usual. Lots of paperwork. Nothing to complain or get excited about either. You?"

Jaye leaned forward over the table, trying to tune out the hustle and bustle around them. If he worked to focus only on the sound of Kris's sweet, smooth voice and the faint scent of his cologne, Jaye could almost pretend they had some privacy. Under the table, he nudged Kris's foot and tried to get him to grin.

"It was good. Normal. Not too busy. Layla surprised me with a cupcake after my shift was over and sang Happy Birthday. It was crazy thoughtful of her." He left out he parts about Mark making things tense. Whenever Jaye mentioned things like that, Kris would urge him to quit and find a new job, but Jaye had worked too hard to climb the ranks at the store to ever think of bailing because of one tight-ass kid. He didn't want to have to start over somewhere new.

Kris got a weird look on his face, a sour smile. "That's a little weird though, right? She's not your girlfriend."

"She's just a nice person. It's not a big deal. She just thought it would be a fun surprise, since I had to work on my birthday and all. Why, you jealous?"

Jaye bit his lip with a sly grin, turning on the charm to draw Kris out, the shyer of the two of them by far. He held Kris's gaze as he tried not to answer, which was totally an answer. Beneath the table, Jaye slid the toes of his right foot up Kris's calf, getting a cute little smile out of him.

"Hey, faggot."

It was just loud enough for them to hear, and came from one of the older guys on the stools, to their right.

"Ignore it," Kris said tightly. He lifted the menu, looking down at it and pulling his leg away from Jaye's foot.

Furious, Jaye had to look around. It figured that as soon as things would start to get good, some loudmouth would ruin it. He was pretty sure the asshole homophobe was one of the barrel-chested guys in hunting gear seated a few feet away.

"Stop looking!" Kris hissed.

But Jaye kept on staring, feeling his anger rising, fast. At first, the big hunters kept their gaze averted. Jaye's fists clenched. His legs tensed. He would have loved nothing better than to spring out of their booth and punch those motherfuckers in the face for throwing hate at strangers who were minding their own business.

One of the guys met his gaze, then held it. He was the one without a beard, or a chin either. It had been swallowed by his neck.

Yeah, that was the guy.

"Jaye!" Kris hissed even more sharply, then kicked him under the table.

Finally turning around, Jaye grumbled, "Maybe we should go."

"No. We're celebrating. We've been planning on this all week," Kris said stubbornly. "Let's just order, then I'll give you your present."

"You got me something?" Jaye asked, brightening the slightest bit. He hadn't wanted to get his hopes up that Kris would be into doing the present thing. He was hit or miss with those kinds of sentimental gestures. On Christmas, Jaye had given Kris a novel he'd wanted to read for months, but Kris hadn't given Jaye anything. He'd said their daytrip to the coast was his gift, even though they'd split the travel expenses right down the middle. Kris hadn't wanted to go, but since he'd let Jaye sway him, he'd spent money he hadn't intended to.

But, whatever. Jaye let it go. The past didn't matter anyway. The way he stayed sane was keeping his eye on the future, looking for ways to keep flying higher, like Cora wanted for him.

"Yeah, of course I did." Kris ducked his head to catch Jaye's eye, showing him he was paying attention. "Hey. Ignore those jerks. We're having a good time, right?"

"Right," Jaye agreed, trying on a smile. He liked hearing Kris's worry for him. "When do you have to catch your bus?"

Though Jaye had been planning his birthday night for months, Kris had gotten a single prepaid, roundtrip bus ticket from his family, who lived further upstate, just a couple of days earlier. It had come with what Kris had insisted was an undeniable request that he make the long trek up to visit for a few days over the coming weekend at their expense. As old-fashioned, close-knit and private people, they had never liked that Kris lived in the city and so far away. Whenever they saved enough to send him bus fare, they expected him to follow through, no matter what.

As someone who also appreciated the value of going out of one's way for family, Jaye had no room to argue, as much as it had hurt his feelings.

"Not for a couple of hours. We have time," Kris assured him. "What kind of cake are you gonna order?"

Jaye laughed, wearing a wide smile and looking down at his hands. "Hmm... All of them?"

They placed their orders for a couple of bacon cheeseburgers and Kris gave Jaye his present. It was wrapped in silver paper covered with bursts of fireworks. Inside was a CD for a punk rock band Jaye really liked, and two tickets for a show they'd be playing at in a couple of weeks.

"This is awesome. Thank you," Jaye told Kris, trying somehow to not lunge across the table and kiss his boyfriend like his whole heart wanted to do. It was better not to attract more unwanted attention.

They didn't have any more trouble with the guys on the stools, who stuck around nursing a couple of beers.

After cake—double chocolate fudge, since they were out of pistachio—and singing, they said goodbye in front of the diner. The golden glow pouring out of the diner's many windows helped Jaye pretend it was warmer than it was. There was still an hour until Kris had to catch his bus, but it wasn't enough time to really do anything else. Their apartment was in the opposite direction, so they couldn't have made the trip there and back. It was far too cold to wander around and Jaye's sore feet couldn't stand the thought of more unnecessary walking anyway, even if it meant being with Kris a little longer. Kris gave Jaye a brief kiss and a hug, whispering against Jaye's cheek, "Love you. Happy birthday. I'll call you once I'm on the bus, okay?"

"Okay. Love you, too. Miss you already."

"I know. I'm sorry again about the timing," Kris apologized.

"Hey, don't sweat it. Thanks for dinner and my present. You're the best. Have a safe trip."

Glancing back over a shoulder, Kris waved as he started to walk toward the bus stop. The wind tossed his hair again, blowing it back from his handsome face like he was in some glossy advertisement. The light shining from the diner's windows cast deep shadows over Kris's angular features. Set against the black sky, with crisp white snow scattered underfoot on the sidewalks, he looked almost like a painting, he was so beautiful. It was an image that stayed with Jaye for the rest of his life.

That was the last time Jaye ever saw him.

Chapter 3
Blindsided

It was a lonely, uncomfortable walk home. The wind whistled in his ears, sounding like eerie, howling voices, chasing after him and hurrying him along faster than his aching feet wanted to go. Jaye went to bed shortly after getting home, figuring it was better to catch up on sleep instead of replaying the train wreck of a day over in his head or listening to the silence of his apartment without Kris there to keep him company.

Jaye had been hoping they'd have time to sneak in a stop back to the apartment before Kris had to leave, maybe give them a chance to screw around a little. It had been months since they'd last had sex. Part of it was work schedule difficulties, exhaustion, or stress related. Those were more excuses than the actual cause of the sexual drought. The real issue was that Kris wasn't big on anal. He was mostly a blowjob kind of guy, which Jaye could work with, usually. Jaye was a big fan of anal, which he realized more and more since having to do without. Doing without wasn't a deal breaker, but leverage like birthdays only came around so often. He'd been hoping to use it to get some, finally.

It wasn't mean to be.

Since Kris had made the daring choice to break away from his family in order to make a better living and follow his own path, the guilt was something Jaye knew he still wrestled with. And it wasn't just guilt about the move. Kris's family didn't know he was gay, or living with a lover. Fear of them finding out, or even just having them suspect he was keeping something from them, had been enough to build a wall between Jaye and Kris. The longer they were together, the more Kris seemed to act like he was having second thoughts about the whole course his life had taken. A private, pessimistic part of Jaye worried each time Kris left to visit his family that it might be a one-way trip.

But Jaye knew that was paranoia talking, and that Kris really did love him in his own way. Without being able to fight the mental battles Kris dealt with, Jaye knew he could only show support and give Kris reasons to be content instead of doubtful. Maybe if Kris wasn't so quiet, and talked more about what bothered him, they would have had a better chance of figuring out a solution together. Jaye knew he had to keep trying, showing Kris how happy they could be if he just let go and relaxed a little.

When Kris—who was sometimes forgetful about promises, as his family's impatience with him seemed to prove—forgot to call Jaye from the bus, he wasn't surprised. Making a mental note to call Kris in the morning to make sure he got in okay, Jaye jerked off in the bed he usually shared with Kris, imagining the anal he wasn't getting. He fell asleep soon after.

The blow to his head was a jarring, disorienting flash of pain between periods of unconsciousness. It was the peaceful blackness of dreamless sleep, followed by an explosion of agony and panic, then a different kind of blackness sank down around him as multiple sets of hands yanked roughly at his body.

More swelling pain and bitter, brutal cold were what brought him back to full awareness.

"Stay still!" he heard. "Yeah, you tried to fucking run, didn'cha? But we've got ya now. Ain't gettin' away again."

The ground beneath him was hard, rough, icy, and scratched at his skin. When he tried to move, he found he couldn't, he didn't budge an inch, which only made him fight harder to try to get free. A hard punch across the side of his head had him seeing stars, but it chased away the rest of his sleepiness. His leaden eyelids managed to lift.

There was a barrel-chested, beardless, chinless man straddling Jaye's bare legs. Jaye's pants and underwear had been removed. They lay in a pile by the man's side. Jaye's arms were being pulled up straight above his head, and were tangled in his shirt, which someone else was sitting on, effectively pinning him in two spots. There was fabric in his mouth, wadded up and shoved between his jaws.

"Kinda like when they run a little at first, though," the guy on Jaye's arms said in a slimy, eager voice. "Makes it more fun to hunt 'em down."

Screaming as hard as he could, he tasted cotton and heard the muffled sound, not nearly loud enough to draw much attention or help. Darkness surrounded them. There were no street lights. As his eyes slowly adjusted, he tried to look around. There was a dumpster to his left, much like the one he'd tossed his mother's garbage in earlier.

He knew where he was. They were in the alley behind Jaye and Kris's apartment building. The night was silent except for that moaning, whipping, icy wind, and had a desolate, hollow feeling. No one else was around.

There was firm, disturbing, unwanted pressure against Jaye's asshole. Then something pressed through it, going inside him, and he instinctively bucked as much he could with his legs and arms trapped, his yells climbing in pitch.

"Little faggot's gonna squeal. Gonna squeeeeeal," the thick, pale man on Jaye's legs taunted. Jaye saw the man's left arm was reached up between Jaye's legs. That was what he felt. The wriggling inside his sphincter was the man's fat fingers.

The more Jaye tried to writhe and fight to get free, to get the fingers out, the more his bare ass scraped on the cold asphalt beneath him, abrading the skin. The steam of his breath fogged the air. He tried somehow to see more, to understand.

"Do it, Burt," the one on Jaye's arms coaxed. "Teach him."

Burt's hand jab-jab-jabbed up into Jaye's ass, pushing up it with rough determination. A cold sweat broke out over Jaye's body the more his position sank in. He was trapped. Shivering and grunting, his chest tightened with his climbing panic, like there was a fist squeezing his lungs, or ropes winding around his ribs, slowly crushing them. He needed to think, to figure out how to get loose, get away. The pressure on his knees, in his rectum, and in his chest were the main problems. He tried to spit out the fabric in his mouth, but couldn't. He tried to free his tangled arms, and couldn't. The night's air caressed his exposed dick and balls, then blew across his stomach. Jaye shivered hard, the cold seeping in past his skin, into his muscles and bones, stiffening them up as he began to freeze.

Those fingers were the most awful thing he'd ever felt in his whole life, stuck in there whether he wanted them or not. He hated how humiliated, weak, and vulnerable it made him feel. He could twist and writhe to show he didn't like it, but those meaty fingers stayed buried, poking around in his passage as his butt cheeks clenched uselessly around them.

"Look at him go!" the one on his arms said happily. "Look at him dance! He fuckin' loves it."

The man sitting heavily on his legs — Burt — looked Jaye in the eye and said earnestly, "Faggots like you love to feel things sticking way inside here, don'cha? You like that? You like to get poked? You're a fucking monster. You know what we do to monsters? Little faggoty ones like you? We give 'em what they want!"

Burt let out a high-pitched giggle that made Jaye's skin crawl, his near-frozen balls trying to draw farther up inside his body for protection.

"Do it, Burt! Do it!" the man by Jaye's arms said, bouncing a little. Jaye quickly tried to pull his arms free and got them slipped slightly out of his shirt, but not nearly enough. The guy sank down onto his shirt again, keeping him pinned.

Jaye told himself to be patient, to wait. He just needed to bide his time and wait for his opportunity.

There has to be one. There has to. It can't end like this.

Burt reached behind his back and pulled something out of his belt. He held it up for Jaye to see and grinned.

Jaye shrieked with all of the air in his lungs, starting to sob, to plead shamelessly, still twisting on those poking, burrowing fingers, the asphalt scraping away more of the skin of his bare butt cheeks.

In Burt's hand was a huge knife, nearly a foot long, but narrow. It was a filleting knife, the kind fishermen used to slice their catch in half or remove its bones.

"Gonna slice open your belly. Pull your insides out. Make you watch."

Slowly, without any hurry and wearing a big, hungry grin, his pink tongue stuck out the side of his mouth like he was concentrating really hard, Burt lowered the blade, point down.

Jaye shrieked again until his voice shredded apart, understanding what was about to happen. He watched as the point of the blade pierced the skin of his side, feeling the pinch almost like a paper cut, but a thousand times more painful. As the blade sank into his stomach, he could feel it inside him, intruding into somewhere it was never meant to be, and at first it didn't hurt much. The skin around the blade stung, but the cold, pure shock of the knife pushing through him was jolting — a focused, direct charge of an electric shock, or a bucket of ice cold water that had him shaking uncontrollably, fighting to breathe. Then, the actual sensations began to kick in, swelling and overtaking him. A dull throbbing blossomed into agony, making him panic. There was no understanding that kind of pain. It was bigger than everything, the reality and the idea both equally horrific. The blade sank deeper, and deeper, and deeper and he couldn't stop looking at it going through him. He wanted to puke and a different kind of cold had him trembling violently. The knife split muscle, carved through organs and cut right through his body until the shocking, stinging agony was mirrored in Jaye's back, as the blade had gone all the way through.

He was completely impaled on the filleting knife.

He was dying

This is dying, he realized.

He urged death on, hoping it would be fast, that it would come and end him so he didn't have to feel the pain anymore. Thrumming in their hold, gasping for oxygen, shrieking and shouting, Jaye could do nothing to stop it.

But the most nightmarish day of his life kept happening. Even the reaper refused to spare him torture, and the pain was unspeakable, frying him from inside out. It loosened ties in his brain, unraveling important instincts and splitting basic mental supports. He didn't have any voice left but he couldn't stop trying to scream the torment. Mostly, he grunted and whimpered around the soaking fabric, his body constantly shaken with slight spasms as tears rolled down either side of his face.

From far away, he heard, "Stuck it right in, just like you wanted me to, didn't I?"

There was more pressure on his asshole as a third finger was stuffed into it, but it didn't matter. Nothing mattered except that blade spearing his side, the handle sticking out but the whole rest of the blade still in his body. The point scraped the ground beneath him whenever Jaye moved.

"Next," Burt said with an eager gleam in his beady, black eyes, "I'm gonna slide ol' pokey right up in here, where my fingers are. It's gonna go in really easy. All it takes is *one push* to stick it in fresh meat like you."

"Pull it out! I wanna see him bleed!"

Burt ignored his buddy and kept talking to Jaye. "Now, I haven't decided if I'm gonna fuck you *before* or *after* I stick my knife in here. Maybe I'll do both! But I do know what I'm gonna do *first*," Burt explained.

Grunting with effort, he buried most of his hand in Jaye's ass, pushing until his fingers were sheathed to the last knuckle, stretching him out wider than he'd been in half a year. The intimacy of the ache added an awful, disgraceful sort of embarrassment to his dying moments. Not only were they going to kill him, they were going to completely emasculate him first. Simultaneously, Burt got a good hold on the knife's handle. Shuddering hard, Jaye sobbed, pleading wordlessly behind his gag, shaking his head back and forth. Burt murmured, "Shhh..." and eased the knife back out.

The well-sharpened blade sliced its way back through his torso. Jaye felt the drag of the edge splitting more of his skin on his back and stomach, carving him up inside, too. It pulled out red.

Blackness rushed in the sides of Jaye's vision as hot wetness began to ooze from his stomach and back.

Stay awake. You sleep, you die.

Jaye cried, whining pitifully, his voice ravaged, able to form only the ghosts of the screams he made before as the gash in his left side was left empty. The blood seeping out went from a trickle to a gush. He stared down at the sight of it, disbelieving, wanting to die, hoping to die, as Burt dropped the knife beside Jaye, then stuck his fingers through the gash and into Jaye's abdomen.

The pressure was maddening, unspeakable. He was being ripped apart. Thrashing violently, shrieking with primal horror and excruciating pain with all of the strength in his body and fighting desperately against that reaching around in his guts, Jaye tried to black out. He willed it, wanting the darkness of oblivion back, but it wouldn't come.

The sensory overload of his nightmare was too powerful to allow him the comforting numbness of unconsciousness.

"Just need..." Burt grunted, reaching around with the first two fingers of his right hand pushed through the parted flesh of Jaye's stomach. The area bulged as Burt pushed and grabbed at Jaye's guts. "To grab hold of one of these ropes, start pulling 'em out, like a magic trick. Gonna pull your guts out, faggot. You wanna see? You're gonna. Gonna take a while to pull 'em all out, too. Gonna be a big pile of your intestines, right over here, when I'm done. After I get a good hold of 'em, it'll just take a second for me to sit you on my dick, ride your faggoty ass while we pull your guts out. That's what we do to monsters like you."

A ghost whispered, right by his ear, *Pay attention.*

Pay attention? Jaye echoed to himself, feeling delirious. His voice was shattered, his energy draining. Everything was cold horror and pain.

After a second, he understood.

The man kneeling on Jaye's shirt was paying attention to Burt's gruesome little speech, not Jaye's arms. The pressure on his arms had eased. Jaye knew he only had one chance. Just one. And it was slim.

He slipped his arms out, as fast as he could, ignoring the pain and those fingers shoved through the peeled open skin of his belly, ignoring how much he needed to die, and grabbed the huge knife that had been dropped at his left side.

He didn't think.

He just acted.

Gripping the handle with both hands, he went for his target. It was one deep slice. A red smile, ear to ear.

One moment it wasn't there, then it was. The smile on Burt's face was mirrored with the one on his wide, swollen neck, just before all of his blood began to pour out in a crimson spray.

Eyes going wide, mouth fallen open in surprise, Burt fell back. His hands slipped out of Jaye's stomach and his ass. The guy by Jaye's head stood up, shouting wordlessly with shock, making weird, primal hooting noises.

Burt grabbed for his throat, trying to hold the blood in, but it was coming out too fast. It was everywhere.

They killed you. They need to pay. They need to be stopped, or they'll do it again, to someone else.

Jaye felt pulled to the second man. Nothing else mattered other than killing him. Nothing.

Pushing on his wound, Jaye lunged with the knife. Stumbling to his feet, expecting to die, ignoring the shock of what he felt, he just went.

The stocky, bearded guy ran down the pitch blackness of the alley, stumbling over his feet and weaving a little, still hooting in fear. Jaye knew the area well, and how the alley ended in the brick wall of the back-end of the one of the buildings in the labyrinthine housing complex, which you couldn't see until you were right up on it, due to the lack of lighting. He often saw cars try to drive down there only to have to reverse all the way back out to the road.

Jaye chased his attacker, throwing himself forward with every step. His body felt heavier with each movement, but it didn't matter. Finishing it was more important than how he felt.

Jaye closed the distance very slowly, the space between them seeming to stretch like taffy. His body felt like it was dragging him down, wanting to crumple when he needed it to *move*.

When the man realized his mistake, that he was trapped, he tried to run back toward Jaye and around him.

Blackness at the edges of things narrowed Jaye's focus, sliding inward.

He finally bridged the gap as the guy flew past and, with an animalistic growl of rage, plunged the blade into his attacker's back, all the way to the hilt.

The man kept running, trying to reach behind him and grab the knife, but was unable to. The handle slipped from Jaye's grasp, left embedded in the man's back. Adrenaline kept him chasing the guy back up the alley, toward the main road, past Burt lying in a dark pool of both their blood.

Jaye did crumple, then, as the pain grew bigger than awareness and turned out the lights for good. But that was okay. He had finished.

Chapter 4

Scarred

Through the haze of painkillers and procedures, surgeries and the long, solitude of recovery, Jaye understood he'd lived, or perhaps, rather, came back. Life kept happening, even if he didn't want it to.

There were no familiar faces to keep him anchored, just unknown nurses, doctors, and police officers. He didn't care to learn their names, so they were an endless parade of strangers who didn't care who he was either or why he was there.

The hardest thing to handle was how things just kept happening. There was no end. It just went on, even though he was done.

Breathing hurt. Moving was out of the question.

The healing process was purgatory, and the way the police presence didn't go away told Jaye that Hell was simply waiting for him to pass on through and join the real party.

He didn't look at clocks or calendars. Time meant nothing to him. There was only sleep, or pain.

The more coherent he felt, the more he was tempted to search and hope for a friendly, familiar face at his bedside when he'd wake. Each time he opened his eyes, and saw nothing, no one, that hope twisted the invisible knife he could still sometimes feel spearing his torso, killing him more.

The attack wasn't the biggest nightmare. The empty chair at his bedside hurt more than anything Burt had done in that alley.

His mom wasn't there. Kris wasn't there. Even Layla wasn't there.

A Get Well Soon card appeared miraculously one day, with a white flower printed on the front and, signed inside, Layla's name and the message, 'My thoughts and prayers are with you.'

Thoughts and prayers, but no people. No family. No friends.

Had Cora OD'd that night of his birthday? Was she not there because she was dead or just trying to be with the help of her addiction, out of guilt or fear?

Once he bothered braving the pain by reaching for his phone, he read the solitary text message from Kris, the only evidence he'd tried to reach out.

It read only, maddeningly, "I'm sorry."

Sorry the message wasn't longer? Sorry Kris was too much of a pussy to show his face? Sorry Jaye had died? Sorry he'd been brutalized?

No answers were there to be found, and none came with time.

There was a record, also, of Cora trying to call Jaye's phone the morning after he'd been attacked, but she didn't pick up or respond to his calls whenever he tried to reach her.

It wasn't worth screaming or crying over. He just used the hurt to numb himself.

It was just Jaye, the carved ruin of his body, and the violated ache of everything in him that had been sweet and innocent. He needed them so much, always had, and to not have them there to help him through his nightmare forced him to close down and shut off.

He slept as often as he could. The nurses and doctors only wanted to touch the parts of his body he least wanted them to.

When his lack of trying to move or recover the ability to resume normal activity caused a bedsore, which became infected, he was transferred to a convalescent center in another part of downtown Anchorage. Everyone there was old, infirm, or overworked. It was always either too quiet or too noisy and smelled terribly, the room he stayed in ancient and worn, like the rest of world had forgotten it, too.

Every day was a struggle between not wanting to move or think, or wanting to avoid another bedsore. Some days he gave up. Others he tried to move, to get back on his feet, or to try *again* to call Cora or Kris. Once, he got Layla on the phone, but it was an awkward, stilted conversation. He could tell she didn't know what to say, or how much to ask, and didn't really want to go to the creepy institution where he was staying, so he gave in and stopped bothering her.

Charges were filed. A court-appointed lawyer in a cheap, pit-stained, ill-fitting suit began visiting him. The lawyer was an over-weight, harried man of about fifty named Lou Meekum. Mr. Meekum had a comb-over and was always chewing gum. He assured Jaye that given his young age and the nature of his crime, he had nothing to worry about. It would be a piece of cake, Mr. Meekum said. What Jaye had done to his attackers was clearly self-defense.

It helped Jaye find a glimmer of hope again. The question of where to go once he was released began to form at the edges of his thoughts. Where would he live? Could he get his job back? Did he even want it anymore? He tried working harder at his rehabilitation exercises to regain his strength. The loneliness left him dispirited enough to keep him quiet and introspective, unsure what was in store for him, or what to do when he was released. Would it be county jail? Would he be set free, then left to track down Cora, to find out if Kris had kept his things or let the lease on their apartment lapse? Maybe everything he owned was already with Goodwill. The lack of good options was daunting, keeping his focus turned inward instead, on the day to day instead of the larger picture.

The trial happened.

It was quick – bewilderingly so.

Through the mind-numbing daze of his powerful painkillers and constant wrong twist in his side, he got the gist. For the first court appearance, he was wheeled in riding a wheelchair. By the second, he was using a cane and moving very slowly, merely shuffling forward with tiny steps.

Mr. Meekum was spineless and exhausted. The judge and prosecuting attorney both only seemed to fixate on his large tattoo and grim demeanor when they saw him. When the prosecution argued against the stance that Jaye was only defending himself, they quickly surmounted the underpaid attorney fighting too limply for Jaye's freedom. Wanting to speak up for himself, but not knowing how to, Jaye was left frustrated and helpless as his likelihood of avoiding prison dwindled away.

It was the running that had done him in. The chasing after the second attacker, Earl Humphrey, who was alive somewhere, nearby, and recovering. Earl had run, and Jaye had chased after him, so the courts said it wasn't self-defense.

Jaye was found innocent of killing Burt McCurdy. They sentenced Jaye to two years in prison for assault with a deadly weapon. Mr. Meekum told Jaye that because Alaska did not have any federal prisons; he would be transferred from the Anchorage Correctional Complex to serve out his sentence at the Federal Corrections Institution in Sheridan, Oregon.

When they snapped on the handcuffs for the first time, Jaye felt it, how he wasn't the same person as he'd been. After so many weeks on his own, trying to hope less and less for the support of someone who cared so his broken heart could begin to mend along with his body, Jaye truly felt detached. He was no longer connected to anyone. There was no one waiting for him to explain what was going on, or asking how he felt about it. His ability to keep going, to fight to get up in the morning and make it through the days without knowing how they would end, all came from within. When the terror of his situation overwhelmed, it was only his own murmured assurances he heard. He dried his own tears. He steadied himself whenever he began to fall.

At first, it was worse than the pain of his wounds, and the fear that came before dying. The long steadiness of the voids created in Cora and Kris's absences ate away at him. But nothing lasted forever and the solitude was reliable in a way Jaye depended on. He had always been willing to fight for himself to get where he needed to go. Now, he would have to do more of the same. Others had failed him, but Jaye refused to fail himself.

He was something else now. Like a phoenix burned down to ashes and dust, then rose again in flames of pure determination, he was a different creature entirely. He wasn't the teenager who had worked as the manager of Rick & Pine, had an apartment with his boyfriend, Kris, and had a junkie stripper for a mom. He was prisoner number 48321. Jaye Larson had died in that alley. Whoever had awoken in his place was someone else, and he wasn't sure yet exactly who it was.

Chapter 5
A & O Status

The Anchorage Correctional Complex was situated in a disturbingly picturesque setting, backed by snow-capped mountains sprawled generously across the horizon line and ringed with leafless trees. It tucked into the rolling landscape like a cozy retreat rather than a gateway to Hell. During the trial, this was where Jaye stayed. He went there directly from the convalescent center. He was booked—a process involving a visual inspection and a pat-down before being handcuffed, followed by an uncomfortably invasive interview with a medical staff member whose name Jaye didn't care to learn. After passing that, he was booked into the facility, questioned on his identification, fingerprinted and photographed. Then, he was taken to a room where he was strip-searched and issued jail clothing before being assigned his temporary housing.

It was a small facility, so he had sensed even before Mr. Meekum eventually clued him in that it wouldn't be his permanent home for the duration of his sentence.

Following a series of disparaging once-overs by the folks in charge, Jaye was brought to his own cell away from the other inmates, who were kept lumped together in larger rooms.

When he asked, "Why am I in here on my own?" the guard sneered and said with a dry chuckle, "Trust me, little girl. If I brought you down there with the men, they'd eat you alive like you were dessert."

Solitude continued to plague him, even in jail. He rarely saw anyone else, and then only the guards and the occasional inmate either being led to another isolation cell or wheeling a food or book cart.

Overpowering dread, expanding in size and strength daily, made him quiet. He only spoke when it was absolutely necessary. He avoided eye contact, went where he was told, and stayed wound tight, ready to snap at the slightest additional stressor or threat.

Once he was sentenced, he was evaluated for placement. Though he wasn't ever given an explanation for the reasoning behind their decision, Jaye figured it was the extremely violent nature of his crime and his crumbling mental state that led them to assign him to a medium security facility rather than a minimum or low security camp.

Due to the extent of his injuries and his recovery time, the reality of what the next two years were going to be like didn't really hit Jaye until he was being transferred from the Anchorage Correctional Complex to FCI Sheridan, Oregon. On the plane, then the bus, loneliness stopped being the concern it had been for so long. He was surrounded by other male inmates, and almost all of them were bigger than him, and looked much more able to kick or tear into his ass. They were all much older than him and were generally terrifying.

Jaye knew he was pretty, and not in a manly way. His pair of tattoos—the bluejay wrapping his back, shoulder, neck and chest, and the tribal piece on his lower abdomen—didn't do much to toughen up his image with grown men baring their own, sometimes plentiful ink. He was slender, with slightly muscular shoulders, a fairly defined chest, and a boyish figure. His dark hair which, even when dry and curly, fell to his lower back, only shelved him more firmly in the category of imminently fucked. Basically, if you squinted, he could pass for a woman.

He had a girly face, girly hair, and a slim body. It didn't matter that he'd recently, gruesomely killed one guy and stabbed another. The only thing that mattered to lonely inmates was how feminine he looked.

For the past few years, he'd been perfecting the art of seducing his customers in order to make a sale, or flying under the radar of his neighbors so they wouldn't give him a hard time for being a teenager living alone with another teenager. Politeness and charm wasn't going to get him *anywhere* anymore.

In transit, he started to get looks, not only from the other inmates, but from the guards as well. Their gazes would drift his way, then stick, and nothing he could do — stare back, ignore it — made the staring stop. It was like they were all imagining the ways he was about to be torn apart by the ruthless convicted criminals he was going to be locked up with. Or else, they were planning the ways *they'd* tear him apart.

His side throbbed as he sat there, trying not to care about the attention. The pain from his injuries was a constant reminder that he couldn't drop his guard, even for a second, not even to sleep. The last time he'd done that, he'd been killed. In the hospital, then in the convalescent center, and finally in his isolation cell in Anchorage, he'd been under guard, so it had been possible to sleep.

Not anymore.

Jaye had accepted it as fact, ever since leaving the hospital, that he had died.

When someone died, they abruptly lost contact with the other people who had been in their life. They traveled far away to somewhere they'd never been and couldn't imagine, taking nothing along with them for the journey but memories.

It made it easier, knowing he was dead. More than anything, actually, it was a comfort.

So, he carried the ache from those fingers, wriggling around in his guts, trying to pull the slick, bloody loops of his intestines out through the new hole sliced into his skin. The memory of his murder was his constant, which he relived over and over again. It had become familiar. He could deal with it.

It was harder to deal with the other sort of ache, since it was only in his head.

No matter where he was, he found, he couldn't stop feeling the fingers Burt had twisted up his ass. They had been the ultimate insult, his greatest shame. Not only had he been dragged from his own bed, then chased into the alley by strangers to be gutted and tossed in a dumpster, they'd needed to punctuate the crime with sexual assault, showing young Jaye exactly how fucked he would always be. He wasn't a person. He was a hole — warm meat that was good to stick things in.

Look at him go! Look at him dance! He fuckin' loves it!

Jaye covered his ears, trying to block out Earl's voice.

You like that? You like getting poked?
You're a fucking monster.

The knife plunged into Earl's back and on the bus, headed to Sheridan, Jaye moaned.

He remembered sitting in the courtroom, surrounded by lawyers, police, strangers, and being anally fingered the whole time. Even as he'd heard his sentence, ghostly hands had been spreading his cheeks and prying at his rim. Wearing a jumpsuit provided by the state, a belly chain with leg irons and sitting on a padded bench as he was bussed to his new home away from home in Sheridan, he was being fingered, too. It never stopped; it only dimmed in his perception now and then.

That ghostly touch was his reminder of what was coming. He knew exactly what the other inmates, hard up and with no access to women, would do to him as soon as they had a chance. When he'd been interviewed about his medical history by an Anchorage Correctional employee prior to sorting, the balding, mustache-clad guy had asked Jaye if he'd been fucked. There had been a look in the man's eye as he'd said it, like a not-so-private joke at Jaye's expense, so Jaye had said the first thing that came to mind in response.

"Lately? Constantly. Night and day. Never gets old."

Good. Get used to it, the man's expression had told him.

So Jaye tried to do just that.

Jaye was going to die again. He felt it. How it would go played out in his head almost constantly, the different scenarios made real in his imagination. Usually what he envisioned was some sort of gang rape that went on for hours before they strangled him to death just to stop his pathetic crying.

In retrospect it was kind of funny, thinking of how often over the past year he'd tried to connive and beg Kris to have sex with him. Sometimes he'd go so far as to climb onto Kris, naked, to put on a show, fingering himself open. Still didn't work. Kris would just jerk off and thank Jaye for the performance with a kiss and a handjob. That was a problem he was no longer going to have, to say the least.

Since Jaye had already died once, he really had no desire to go through it again. So, he began to scrutinize his options. Watching his mother get mistreated her whole life by brutish men had hardened

Jaye in subtle ways to what others might see as romantic or excitingly sexy situations. No, he understood, just as the guy doing his medical history interview had, that sometimes it was just about who was getting fucked.

He could try to fight back, but he couldn't keep doing that with everyone who'd try to test him. There were some men who would always be bigger and stronger. What he needed in order to survive was respect, and that was something he had to fucking *earn*. The bitch of it was that if he kept killing people, even if it was self-defense, they could just keep tacking on more years to his sentence. Then, he'd never get out.

And if there was any goal left to him at all, it was to — someday — get out. To be free, like Cora had wanted for him.

But if he couldn't fight back, what else could he do?

Go along with it?

That was a nauseating, awful idea, which was how he knew it was the right one.

For most of his voyage south, he was preparing himself, mentally, for what he needed to do. He'd have a limited window of opportunity, because if the fucking over started too soon, he might be left maimed, crippled, or simply labeled as damaged goods. Then his plan would never work, and he sure as shit needed it to work.

Starting in the plane, then in the bus, he began to gauge the other inmates. Some had obvious gang affiliations because of visible tattoos. Some were bigger in size, or just had a meaner look about them. Some had a gay vibe, or a creepy vibe, or a scary, avoid-at-all costs vibe. He told himself to trust his gut reactions and practiced his mental categorization of those around him.

On the bus, the guy to Jaye's left didn't have any visible white power ink, though he was definitely Caucasian. The inmate number on his jumpsuit had a C in front of it. Jaye's didn't have any letter at all. Some other guys had B's. He was an older guy and looked like he'd be well at home on a Harley, tearing up asphalt. Going with his best option given the pasty hue of his skin and his slim knowledge of how gangs were typically defined, Jaye knew he had to speak up for himself and seize the opportunity.

"You in with any crews?" Jaye asked the guy under his breath, without any hope of a response other than a nasty look or an obscene remark.

The guy gave him the side-eye and sniffed. His gaze drifted low, to Jaye's lap, then back up again. "The Disciples," he said, in a gravelly, gruff voice.

"They at Sheridan?"

"They're fuckin' everywhere, princess," he laughed. Some others nearby joined in. "Sweet young piece of pussy like you... you lookin' for a man to belong to?"

"Maybe. Who leads your crew?"

The guy laughed even harder.

"Oh, you wouldn't like him. Cash might be younger than me, but he's been through the meat grinder more times than I can count. Made him mean. Made him *ugly*. Made him able and willing to do whatever the fuck he's gonna do."

"How the hell do you know? You been in Sheridan?"

"Two times, sugar. Third's the charm, I guess."

"Bet Cash gets some fuckin' respect, though," Jaye said, sitting up a little straighter, keeping his voice low enough not to attract attention from the guards.

"Bet your ass he does."

Jaye ran it through his head, trying to find his *in*, his way to stay alive.

Taking a chance, and likely a stupid one, he said, "Look, I can suck a cock better than anyone in that whole fucking facility. If you tell me how to find Cash so I can make him my man, that's gonna make you look good. Really good. Bet he'd be real fuckin' grateful you hooked us up. What's your name?"

"Ro," the old biker with short, salt and pepper hair said, looking at Jaye more thoughtfully now.

"What do you say, Ro? Wanna look real fuckin' good in front of your boss? Have him give you a warm welcome back?"

Ro chuckled, clicked his tongue against his teeth and shook his head. "Can't say no to that, can I? You got some smarts, kid. Almost makes me feel bad about what's gonna happen to you once you're locked inside. Boss man's in Unit 4. Big bald motherfucker who looks like he's been to war and back more than a few times and covered in head-to-toe tattoos. You see a group of white guys together without any swastikas on their foreheads? That's the Disciples. The guy in the center of the pack? That's the boss man."

"Thanks, Ro."

"No sweat. Think of me when you've got a mouthful of his dick, huh?" He laughed again.

"I'll do better than that if you help me get to him. I need to find him today, as soon as possible. Otherwise for all I know I could be dead by morning. They're going to separate us out, right? We won't be with the others already inside for a while. If there's an opening to have a face-to-face talk with Cash, would you help me make it happen?"

"How?"

"I don't know."

"Like a distraction?" Ro shifted his sleeve and something small slipped down into his palm. He caught it between his index and middle fingers. It was a matchbook. "Got a smoking habit," he explained. "So, look. The section of the prison where they'll be taking us new guys is known for being understaffed. New inmates might want to escape, but the last thing they're likely to do is try to get *further into* the prison. They're mainly watching the exits, less so the halls connecting one unit from the next. They might put one guard on hall monitoring, but any major activity will get him to come runnin'. Unit 4 guards patrol the inside. The doors are set up so you can get in whenever you want, but you can't get out without a passkey."

"Okay," Jaye nodded, filing it all away in his head. "How do you know all of this?"

"Guy in our crew went after a target in a rival gang right after entry a couple years back. He got thrown in ad-seg for it once they caught him, but they didn't bother changing policies. What do they care if we kill each other? Just means less work and expense for them." Jaye felt the bus turn sharply, all of the men inside leaning to the left to compensate for the shift. "So, little lady, if I do this... what's my thank you for a favor this big?"

"If I talk to Cash, I'll let him know he owes you. If not, I'll thank you myself, any way you want."

"You better. You don't come through on this, I'll pull out each one of those nice white teeth myself so you're an even better cocksucker than before. You get me?"

"Yeah. Got it."

As they pulled off of the main road and rolled up to FCI Sheridan, Jaye's mental wheels started to turn. He had to pay attention, stay on his feet. Everyone he saw was going to be chewed up and fed into the machine. Jaye psyched himself up for it, focusing his mind, figuring out everyone he laid eyes on based on gut instinct alone and keeping the plan in mind. He fed on the pain in his body to keep him sharp, and told himself it was do or die in a very literal sense.

Chained together, they were all led into the building. Uniformed men with guns lined the walls. More of them waited inside. The new arrivals were led into a long room and introduced to the Receiving and Discharge Technician, who was accompanied by a medical staff member in scrubs and a white coat. They were un-cuffed and told to strip down. Jaye cupped his genitals in his hands, his eyes forward, focused on no one in particular as he braced himself for anything. One by one, the guy in scrubs looked down their throats, between their toes, and under their balls. They were told to bend over, spread their cheeks, and cough. It wasn't really a comfort that everyone had to do it, that it wasn't just him being singled out; it just underlined how powerless Jaye had become, his pride as shredded as the muscles in his side had been by that knife.

They were all given A & O or Admission and Orientation status, which would last until they completed the A & O program and the FCI Unit Teams had compiled sufficient information and documentation for their institutional classification to be completed. After they were issued khaki-colored Institutional clothing affixed with their last name and register number, they were led to another room to complete paperwork, including a summary of their social and medical history, the filling out of identification forms, and the completion of personal property inventories. Lastly, they were issued Institutional bedding and some basic supplies like a toothbrush, toothpaste, and a bar of soap.

They were told that they would be assigned to one of four Housing Units sometime in the following week or two. In the meantime, they would be housed in a separate area for inmates with A & O status. On the way to their housing area, they were led past a hallway leading to a closed recreational area filled with inmates. There was a sign on the wall that read Unit 4. Passing it by, Jaye knew it was almost time. He glanced back to Ro, who nodded slowly, then winked.

As soon as the guard leading them pointed to their housing area, the A & O Case Manager raised her voice, saying loudly to them, "Listen up! Schedules and information on all Admission and Orientation lectures will be posted here on the information post in your assigned area. You are expected to attend all lectures, call-outs and appointments this week and beyond, after you've been assigned to your Housing Unit. You are required to remain in this area. All other areas are Out of Bounds. Any questions?"

There was a general murmur of no, some shaking of heads.

"You're right there," a guard told Jaye, pointing to one of the lower level bunks. It was stripped down to the bare mattress.

"Thanks." He walked over and set down his supplies, orientation handbook and bedding.

"Those of you on the top bunks, you will find a step welded into the bed frame here," the A & O Case Manager yelled, pointing to the nearest bunk. "This is the only safe and approved way to access your bunk."

After a few more announcements, the Case Manager left. The guards were distracted with everyone's milling around. Ro was on the other side of the room, farther away from the door.

The other new arrivals around him were checking out their spaces, getting situated. But Jaye knew he was losing precious time. Bathrooms scared him. Showers scared him. The dining hall scared him. Basically anywhere that wasn't his bunk scared him, but even there, he knew he wasn't safe. One of the other new arrivals, or someone with contacts, could get to him if they wanted to badly enough. Everyone was the enemy.

The prison was medium security. They weren't confined as tightly as they might have been somewhere else. Hell, they even had landscaping and personal trainer classes to help inmates find employment after their eventual release. It was a pretty cushy place.

That was both a good and bad thing. Bad because if he could walk around easily, so could everyone else. But it was good because it gave him his one, slim, desperately needed chance to do what he knew he needed to, to survive.

When someone yelled, "Fire! Yo man, this dude's shit is on fire!" Jaye was ready.

The other inmates in the room surged for Ro and the flames, as did the guards. Jaye edged backward as slowly as he dared, heading for the door. When he felt none of the guards were looking his way, he slipped from the room and went right for Unit 4, right down the hall.

Chapter 6
Meeting with the Mark

"What do we got here?"

"I think she's lonely. Got somethin' to keep you company, sugar."

Unit 4 was packed. Long rows of cells lined the walls on multiple levels. Pinpoints of daylight from the small high windows didn't add much illumination; it was the buzzing fluorescents above that painted the scene in garish, yellowed colors. In the center on the bottom floor, there were grey, rectangular tables with bench seats along with round ones with plastic orange chairs. There were men of all shapes, ages, sizes, and ethnicities but they were all older and more intimidating than Jaye.

He looked for the whites. It seemed most men in the room had migrated toward others of similar skin tones to their own, sorting everyone by ethnicity more obviously than Jaye had ever seen in any other setting. When he located the groups of Caucasians, he looked for the ones without Aryan nation tattoos or hairstyles. Within a matter of seconds, he saw some badass looking guys in a far corner, standing near to one another while making it clear they weren't doing anything that would violate rules and regulations. They didn't have the typical swastikas or triple sixes on their necks. Instead, they had large letter D's and the words 'The Disciples', the numbers twelve or seventy, or large, ornate crosses inked into their areas of visible skin. He tried to hone in on whoever might be in charge.

There was one guy who seemed a good match to Ro's description of his boss. The others around him seemed to be drawn to him instead of each other, giving him a portion of their attention at all times. He looked like he was in his thirties—somewhere around the median age of the group. He was the most ravaged, with more tattoos, brands, and scars than anyone else. He was bald, with a large, thickly muscled body that conveyed plenty of power and confidence. That guy had been through hell, but he wore a calm expression and had no fear at all in the way he carried himself. Everything about him screamed, 'stay away from this guy in particular at all costs.'

That was Jaye's mark.

"Hey sweet thang, lemme get a taste of that! Come on, we don't bite!"

"Got ourselves a *real* lady!"

"Hey chica, don't be shy! Got something for you right here...."

Jaye walked faster, wading through dangerous waters with threats on all sides, circling him like ravenous sharks. As he moved through the men, all eyes turned to fix on his body. The guys who weren't yelling at him just stared silently, and that was somehow even worse. He knew, though, that as soon as he stopped moving, he'd be able to feel the fingers again, more clearly than ever. It wasn't just the outward threats that drove him on.

Sure, he was scared out of his mind, but it wasn't like he had a choice or any better options. Remembering how it had felt to chase down his attacker with a bloody knife in hand, he just kept going. Mentally, he went back there, wore his need like a cloak, hardened himself, and chased his target like he'd chased Earl.

His mark was watching him.

Jaye got pretty close, within maybe twenty feet, before the guys lower on the gang's hierarchy stepped in to block his way.

One of the guys looked like an old hippie, with long, flowing hair, almost as long as Jaye's, and a long beard to go with it. The other was hairy in a rougher, furrier way, and built like he was the muscle of the group, bigger than anyone else around, though Jaye didn't like the look the guy gave him, as if Jaye's baby face was turning him on in a big, pedophilia way. "Whoa, baby, that's close enough. What'chu need, sweet cheeks? Whatever you need I—"

"I want to make a deal. With you. Just you." He pointed at his mark, looking at no one else. As an afterthought, he added, "Ro told me how to find you."

Jaye tossed his hair back, and, like his life depended on it—which it did—he poured sex into his expression like he'd never, ever done before. It was a glint in his eyes, the shape of his mouth, and his body language. He hooked his thumbs in his waistband and tugged at it a little to show a flash of inked skin.

One of the guards noticed what was going on and stepped forward. He looked like he was in his thirties, with short, dull brown hair and attentive, intelligent brown eyes.

"We got a problem here?" the guard asked. His name tag read, 'Dorrance,' and he used his baton to push back some of the gang members who had advanced on Jaye.

Too slow. Too late. You're fucked.

There was an awful moment where nothing happened, and Ro's boss, Cash, didn't do a single thing to let on he was the least bit interested. Jaye could feel how doomed he was. They'd eat him alive and laugh as they carved him up.

A flicker of this terror moved through his expression, briefly.

"Just having a conversation. No problem at all," Cash said. He stepped forward and the rest of the guys stepped back, just like that.

Dorrance looked between Jaye and Cash. Jaye stepped forward, closer to Cash's side and Cash smiled at Dorrance.

The guard nodded and backed off, but kept watching the pair of them.

"What kind of deal?" Cash said, quietly, without looking directly at Jaye but only playing it cool.

"I wanna be yours. You protect me; I'll suck or fuck you better than you've ever *dreamed,* whenever, however."

Cash laughed. It was a deep, full belly laugh with the guy's rich baritone voice. Jaye saw how Cash's nose and cheekbones had been broken at least once, and had healed crooked. He had cauliflower ear like some MMA fighters Jaye had seen on TV. Maybe, before he'd seen some fucked-up types of war, he'd been good-looking, but not anymore. Now that Jaye had an even closer look, it was clear the guy was *carved* out of muscle. That, and his obvious respect within the prison, were all that mattered. Just the fact that he'd gotten Dorrance to back off instead of hauling Jaye back to A & O spoke loudly.

"What's your name, boy?" Cash asked, glancing at Jaye for only a second, like he didn't care and Jaye was only a passing, annoying amusement.

"Jaye."

"Jaye for what?"

"I-it's just Jaye," he said. His voice faltered, breaking a little as his hope drained out through the bottom of his feet and murky visions of how he'd die this time came back to cloud out reality. It wasn't just Dorrance watching; it seemed the entire room full of hundreds of convicts were salivating, eager to bite off pieces of him.

"Jaye for Johnny?"

Cash looked at him again, a little longer, focusing on Jaye's body instead of his face. He craned his neck to specifically check out Jaye's ass and a creepy shiver raced up Jaye's spine.

"Sure. Johnny." The visual scrutiny gave Jaye goosebumps, his balls drawing up and his heartbeat quickening. Cash could call Jaye whatever the hell he wanted as long as he was interested. Jaye didn't fucking care.

"Let's take a walk, Johnny," Cash said, nodding back toward where Dorrance was standing, and an alcove adjacent to him.

"Okay," Jaye nodded, falling in just behind and beside Cash.

When they left most of the crowd behind, Jaye's heart really started to pound, his mouth drying up and his stomach churning uneasily. Adrenaline had been carrying him through, but shit was getting real now. They stepped into the alcove in Dorrance's line of sight, but out of the view of everyone else except for a few of the mark's buddies who had moved closer to block everyone else's view. In the alcove there was nothing but a locked, grey, metal door. The walls were white, painted cinderblock, marked with some scuffs and grime. The mark backed Jaye up to the solid wall beside the metal door.

"You keep me alive, keep anyone else from touching me, I'll do whatever you want. I'm the best cocksucker you've ever met," Jaye promised, his raspy voice faltering only a little, but enough to show the mark just how petrified he really was, underneath the bravado.

The mark folded his beefy arms over his broad chest, looking Jaye up and down, but focusing mostly on Jaye's lips and his torso. He walked right up to Jaye, until their bodies were almost touching. Jaye yelled at himself to stay fucking still, to man up.

"How'd you know Ro?"

"Sat next to him on the bus. Told him I thought his boss might want someone pretty to keep him company. Give you first crack at owning me."

Cash leaned in to sniff Jaye's neck, just below the side of his jaw. Straightening back up, his finger played with one of Jaye's curls, which tumbled down over his shoulder and down past his chest.

"Turn and drop 'em."

Jaye's heart was in his throat. Trembling, lightheaded, focusing on the pain to lead him through, he turned. All he saw was cinderblock. He intentionally blocked out the imposing human shapes crowding into the edges of his vision. He pushed his pants and underwear down past the curve of his ass. To be exposed like that in a roomful of men who'd all happily line up to rape him was just as maddening as it had been to lie helpless in the alley during his attack. Only now, he was voluntarily putting himself in that position.

Cash shifted closer, bracing his left hand on the roughly textured cement block wall beside Jaye's head. Two big, dry fingers pushed, hard, through Jaye's asshole, going in to the last knuckle and hooking expertly in his body.

It startled him, even if maybe it shouldn't have. More uneasy shivers made his skin pebble. Knowing he had to play the part, he let out a breathy, rough exhale and clenched up as the fingers twisted around and tested him, feeling him out.

"You a faggot?"

The fingers spread apart.

"For you, sure. Just wanna—" his voice caught on a slight whimper as the fingers jabbed hard, going deeper and bending, prying at him. "Wanna keep breathing air. I know how I look. And I'm not a— *ahh*—pussy. I killed a guy. I'd do it again, but I'm loyal. If you own me, then I'm loyal only to you."

The two fingers pulled quickly out. Jaye heard Cash spit and the fingers were replaced with two plus a thumb, covered in a thin film of wetness. The tapered wedge pried at the outer muscle of his rim and his breath caught again. Out of the corner of his eye, he noticed Dorrance watching the whole thing.

Overwhelmed by fear, it caused the air to rush from Jaye on a quaking sigh. His skin contracted from his scalp to his curled toes, fitted inside his ugly state-issued shoes. He shivered even though the air wasn't cold, but humid with the stale breaths of too many men packed into a poorly ventilated space.

"You're tight. Too tight for a whore."

"Not a whore. B-basically a virgin. But I'd be *your* whore."

"You'd do things for me? Be my bitch?"

"Yeah," Jaye grimaced. The prying hurt enough that he had to brace himself on the wall with both hands before his knees gave out. He stuck out his ass a little more, in invitation to the probing, trying to tempt the way he'd done with Kris for so long. The mark's eyes were all over him, judging, and the guard was obviously in his pocket, maybe a pervert, too, but the other Disciples were there. He was just meat again. Something pretty to fuck.

You're a salesman, aren't you? Spent years selling overpriced shit to people who didn't really need to buy any of it. So sell the merchandise. Sell your ass or die.

"Yours. Your bitch."

The mark shoved his hand in farther and spread it apart again, enough to really hurt. Jaye bit off a cry of pain, turning it into a growl, fighting instincts that made him want to protest or fight his way out of there, to make the touching and intimate hurt stop, no matter what. The cool feel of the wall he leaned against was contrasted by the throbbing heat in his sphincter and the flush of shame on his face.

Jaye's knees quivered and he hung his head, trying to breathe normally. He refused to look around and acknowledge the men watching all of this, seeing him beg for more with half of a thug's hand crammed up his ass.

The mark leaned in and whispered, "What's *basically* mean, Johnny?"

"M-means I'd *love* to suck your cock and swallow your load." He mewled through the deepening, intense ache as the mark kept testing him, stretching his asshole until Jaye was up on his toes and panting with little desperate breaths.

Nearby, some of Cash's crew laughed like they were loving the show. Jaye caught a glimpse of the furry crew member eye-fucking Jaye from only a few steps away with a disturbing intensity.

"Fuckin' hurts, huh, bitch?" Cash growled.

"Let me be your property. Your sex slave. You can protect me from them, right? If you keep them off of me, then there's more for you."

"Oh, don't you worry your pretty head about that. What's mine is mime. Is this cherry mine?"

He plucked Jaye's rim, then rubbed over it with three fingers, back and forth, before sheathing them again with a contented hum by Jaye's ear. It made Jaye grunt heavily and bend a little with the force of the push.

"Yes, if we have a deal."

Cash shifted, then came even closer. The fingers pulled out. Cash hocked up some phlegm and spat again. Jaye felt it—the massive, blunt cock pushing hard at his sore, throbbing sphincter. The wide head, which felt as big around as the wrong end of a baseball bat, popped through and Jaye bit at his tongue with a hard, long groan, trying to move past the very real pain causing his knees to weaken and a shrill scream to bubble up in his throat. The mark's hands clamped on Jaye's hips as he began to collapse, pulling him back onto the rest of the huge dick burrowing up his ass.

Jaye couldn't breathe. It was too much, too dry, too thick. With small, terrible whimpers he had no way to hold inside, Jaye clenched in flutters around the thug whose cock was stuffing his ass. Jaye just prayed he hadn't made the wrong call, and this guy wasn't about to signal for his friends to have at him next.

"Think I just felt that cherry pop," Cash laughed. "That hurts, huh?"

Jaye made a frantic little gasp, his hands clawing at the cinderblock.

A big, callused hand rubbed Jaye's right butt cheek, then squeezed the muscle. He gave Jaye a small thrust, inching farther. Jaye grunted, his head swimming, his body in torment, throbbing around that one small point of violation. Another thrust, then he felt his mark's balls brushing him. The cock claiming him felt like it was taking him apart. He had no idea sex could hurt so much, the delicate tissues of his rectum stretched to their limit, gripping something too big to ever have been meant to be inside it.

Trembling, Jaye felt absolutely powerless. He'd done this to himself, but the reality of it pushed his mind into the dark, where nothing was clear but the creeping, crawling, slithering nightmares that lived in shadow. There was no comfort there, only the primal need to survive, somehow.

The whisper of a voice spoke up in his head, the one that had told him to wait in that alley until he had his moment to slip free and act.

Sell it, it said.

He wasn't peddling designer jeans anymore, but making the customer happy now was exponentially more important than it had ever been at Rick & Pine. If he wanted what he was pitching, he had to make it seem like a great deal. It didn't fucking matter if he'd be shitting blood for a week, as long as he was alive to do it.

So, Jaye started to move, just a little circling of his hips. Gently, he clenched up on Cash's dick and shivered. In a seductive rasp, he begged, "Please don't hurt me. Your cock is so fucking *huge*."

A low rumble of a chuckle in Cash's chest was felt more than heard. He started to move counter to Jaye's gyrations, working himself in the tight vise of Jaye's mostly virginal ass.

"Please," Jaye moaned, letting his mark hear how much Jaye was getting turned on, how much he wanted it. "It *hurts*."

He kept fucking himself back onto the guy, doing everything he knew. He glimpsed from the edge of his vision that Dorrance, the furry guy, the hippie and some other members of Cash's crew were watching intently. Some of them were touching themselves through their clothes.

Cash twisted his fist in Jaye's long curls, then pulled, forcing Jaye's head back. Jaye kept his hands braced on the wall, his ass out, his legs spread. Cash withdrew oh-so-slowly, until his head caught on Jaye's aching rim. Then, he hummed, hungrily. "Mmm, look at that."

"Fuck 'im, boss. *Fuck 'im hard*," one of the others goaded greedily.

Once more, Cash spat into his hand. Slightly wetter, the entire shaft plunged back into Jaye, driving him back up on his toes. He was gritting his teeth, grunting through the burning, throbbing ache and breathing hard. The others laughed. Cash sighed in pleasure. He held Jaye still by the hair and the hip, stringing him out and not giving him the ability to shift a fraction of an inch, then began to fuck him hard and fast. That big, wide dick drove into him, pounding his hole. It was all raw friction. Jaye couldn't draw breath, and made frantic, soft pleading noises. Tears were in his eyes when he felt Cash convulse with orgasm.

You aren't at the goddamned shopping center anymore. Man the fuck up! This is your fight, right now, and there's only two options. You want to get fucked, or you want to die bloody and screaming?

When Cash pulled out, tears were on Jaye's face. The terrifying man who'd just force-fucked Jaye saw them before he could wipe them away.

"Look at me, bitch."

Jaye turned, trying to pull his pants back up but fumbling a little, feeling like he was about to pass out. Cash grabbed hold of him by the jaw, then rubbed Jaye's full lips before letting go. He didn't back off.

"You feel that, right? How I'm still fucking that hole? How that's gonna be throbbing for days? And you ain't gonna sit or shit right for a long damn time?"

"Yes, sir," Jaye croaked, feeling jittery and drained. All of his fight was used up.

"That's our deal. That's *my* hole, now. It's mine, not yours. No one else touches it. You do what I say, no matter what it is."

"Always," Jaye promised.

"Someone asks who you are, what do you say? What's your name?"

"J-johnny."

"You know my name?"

"Cash."

Jaye hated the tears that were still on his face, but wasn't sure if he was allowed to wipe them off. He looked at all of those scars and marks. A jagged scar ran down the top of Cash's right cheekbone all the way down the side of his face to his mouth, like the whole side of his face had once been carved open. Another scar ran through his left eyebrow, then jumped down to catch his cheek, just below his eye. He was bald, the hair shaved off instead of missing, since you could see the stubble on top of his head along with the stubble covering his jaw. A brand of the letter D marred the side of his neck, the skin raised and pink. The numbers seventy and twelve had been inked ornately into the top of his head. Three blue, open teardrops cascaded down from his left eye. The mark's eyes were a hard, cool grey-blue and Jaye inexplicably found himself calmed by looking into them.

"That's right. Makes sense, you belong to me. Everyone's gonna know it. So, who are you?"

"Cash's bitch, Johnny."

"Good," Cash praised, with a hint of a smile, looking at Jaye's mouth like he wanted to use it for something dirty. "Guess I have ta thank ol' Ro for the favor, handing me such a pretty piece. Gonna talk to my friends, see about getting you moved in with me. You want that?"

Jaye nodded enthusiastically. If he was with Cash, then he wouldn't have to keep his guard up as much at night. Better the devil you know.

"Good." Cash exhaled a breath and looked out at the other guys, then back at Jaye. More quietly, Cash said, "It won't hurt as much once you get used to it. Okay? First time's the worst."

For a second, Jaye thought he'd misheard, but he'd been so on edge. He'd been wound up and ready to fight for his life since that alley, and to hear even a hint of kindness and reassurance from this guy who didn't know Jaye from Adam or owe him anything....

Jaye's voice caught when he tried to speak. He held his breath, his eyes too wide, too wet, as if he couldn't stop the heartache bleeding out. He'd needed that hint of kindness for months, and to get it in such an unlikely place?

He fought tooth and nail to get it together, but he knew he was making soft, broken sounds. When Cash just shifted a step over to block Jaye from view, instead of laughing or mocking him for being so fucking weak, it only unraveled more of Jaye's inner ties keeping him together.

"S-sorry," he hiccupped. "T-thank you."

He grabbed hold of the front of Cash's shirt to have something to anchor to as he composed himself.

"Take a deep breath. Gonna take you out, show 'em who owns you now."

Jaye nodded and breathed. He wiped his eyes.

After a minute or two, Jaye was more composed but let the others see as much of his physical discomfort as they wanted, since it would just make Cash look better. They left the alcove behind and joined the others. Cash's arm was slung around Jaye's shoulders, dragging him along even though Jaye was walking funny, his arms folded over his chest and eyes downcast.

Everyone nearby turned to look. Cash walked Jaye to the center of where the Disciples were gathered. All of the guards perked up, watching closely. Cash let go and gave Jaye's ass a hard squeeze.

Face flushing red, knowing he looked shaken, Jaye held still while Cash groped him. Chuckling, Cash said, "Hey, I'd like you all to meet Johnny. Keep your fucking hands off him, got it? Especially you, Wolf, I know you've got a thing for the young ones."

"Got it, boss," was the murmur through the nearby guys.

"Gave him a hard ride, huh, boss?"

"Sure fuckin' did, but he can take it, can't you, Johnny?" Cash grinned, palming Jaye's ass.

"Yeah, Cash," Jaye answered obediently, even though his face was still beet red. "I loved it."

"Prettiest bitch in the place, boss," the hippie-looking guy said.

"You know it, Gravy," Cash winked. "And, hey, I fuckin' deserve it, don't I?"

The crew laughed in agreement. Cash hooked an arm around Jaye's neck again, nudging him a little. It was all a blur. Jaye couldn't keep watching out like he had been. It had been too much, too fast, and he was exhausted, just wanting to curl up and wait for the throbbing to stop.

"Hey!" Cash snapped, furious in a flash. "You don't fucking look at him! That's *mine*."

"S-sorry!" Jaye heard. He looked around for whoever Cash had yelled at, and it was a beefy guy with the shoulder span of a linebacker. But at Cash's reprimand, the guy was shaken. "Sorry, Cash."

"You better be fuckin' sorry," Cash warned.

Chapter 7
Purgatory

It had been a huge gamble to approach Cash about the deal without knowing him at all. Jaye had been going on gut instinct, only, but knew he really didn't have any other choice. Meeting Ro had given Jaye the small opening he'd needed to align himself with someone strong and respected. If Jaye had done nothing at all, he would have been guaranteed to get hurt. A slim chance was always better than none at all, especially in life or death situations.

Right after Cash fucked him, Jaye was reprimanded by the guard, Dorrance, and the A & O Case Manager for being Out of Bounds. Probably due to his age, the general air of desperation around him, and his unfortunately feminine appearance, they were letting him off with a warning, but next time it would mean a fine he'd have to work off or pay back. By scrutinizing the looks exchanged between Dorrance and Cash, Jaye realized Dorrance had waited to remove Jaye from the area specifically because of Cash. The two of them had some sort of creepy arrangement, where Cash got away with shit while Dorrance got to watch. There was probably some other deal going on there too, but did it involve drugs, sex, or what?

The new arrivals were supposed to stay in the A & O area until assigned their Unit and introduced into the general population. Semen ran down the inside of Jaye's leg. He had no immediate shower access. He was fucked raw, seriously hurting, and exhausted almost to the point of collapse. In this ragged state, Jaye shuffled back to his bunk accompanied by one of the A & O guards. All of the other new inmates in sight got quiet, staring at him. He didn't care. Curling up on the bare mattress with a groan, palming the mostly healed slash in his side, Jaye stopped fighting for the moment in order to deal with the effects of what he'd done.

The other new arrivals were watching him moan, grimace, and writhe, probably wondering what hell he'd stumbled into not even an hour into arriving in their section. The room was hushed in an uncomfortable, spooky way.

Jaye didn't blame them for being freaked out. He was freaked out, too.

"Hey, man," one of the older, darker-skinned guys said to him, "You okay? What'd they do to you? My name's Henry, by the way."

"I'm fine. No big deal," Jaye said through gritted teeth. "Nice to meet you, Henry."

"Was it the guards?" the guy whispered with an uneasy expression.

"Nope, just me."

Ro was across the room. He wandered a little closer, into Jaye's line of sight. Holding his gaze, Jaye nodded. Seeming satisfied or maybe tired of drawing attention to himself, Ro went back to his bunk.

Their toilet and sink were in the room with them. Jaye knew he had no choice, even though he really didn't want to clean up in front of all those strangers — men who might want to give his ass a ride of their own and wouldn't care the slightest bit about his deal with Cash. But, if he was bleeding, the last thing he wanted was to be walking around with a noticeable blood stain on the seat of his khaki pants.

Everyone was doing a pretty good job of averting their eyes whenever someone went to sit on the pot. But, once it was his turn, and his ass was set on the metal seat after holding out as long as he possibly could, he didn't feel like he had nearly enough privacy.

There was blood, but just a little. He washed it away, along with Cash's come, by splashing water from the sink on his ass and inner thighs.

Unsurprisingly, other guys noticed. Wishing he was invisible or had any other way to avoid their stares, Jaye finally glanced up. A few of them were exchanging looks of shock. Some, instead, gained a predatory, hungry glint to their eyes.

From farther down the long room, barely audible, he heard someone say, "Hey, white boy's giving up his ass."

In response, a gruff voice that sounded a lot like Ro said, "White boy belongs to the boss man of the Disciples."

"Oh."

"You need a medic?" Henry asked from a neighboring bed as Jaye he returned to his cot.

"No," Jaye replied shortly, curling up on his good side and closing his eyes.

Like most of the other inmates with A & O status, Jaye kept to himself as much as possible. Days bled into each other. They were completely segregated from the rest of the prison population, eating separately, showering separately, and kept out of common areas. They stayed in their section until there was what FCI termed a Controlled Movement of all A & O inmates to the dining hall or one of the larger multi-purpose rooms used for lectures. Depending on when they got there, sometimes various religious symbols were propped up against the walls in the lecture room, so Jaye figured it doubled as home for worship services. The mandatory lectures were to explain how FCI Sheridan worked, laying out all of the policies and programs. Jaye tried to soak up as much information from them as he could, no matter how boring they were, just in case. He'd always felt it paid off to be as well-informed as possible, no matter where you were or what was going on.

The nights were noisy and unsettling, but not entirely because he was locked up. There were rules against talking once it was lights out, and for the most part the guys obeyed. But what sounds there were — footsteps, whispering, dripping, bangs, distant buzzing alarms, random shouts — bounced off all of the cold, hard surfaces of the walls, floors and ceilings, traveling farther than they might have otherwise.

Those noises he could account for.

However, Jaye had been having a lot of trouble sleeping ever since Burt McCurdy and Earl Humphrey had dragged him out of his bed. Nightmares were always a guarantee. The insomnia only intensified in prison, since he was never alone, had no way to defend himself against an attack, and could never be sure of the intentions of the strangers with whom he was locked up.

He'd lay there, in the dark, watching for movement and listening.

Sometimes he'd feel Burt touching him, fingering Jaye's ass or reaching into his guts. Jaye would grunt, trying not to physically fight something he knew wasn't really there, as tempting as it was to do so.

I'm gonna slide ol' pokey right up in here, where my fingers are. It's gonna go in really easy.

Shh...

Gonna pull your guts out, faggot.

He heard it clear as day, as if Burt was there, leaning over him. Curling into a tighter ball, Jaye murmured as quietly as he could, "Shut up. Leave me alone. You're not here."

Not having anyone he trusted or knew to talk to, just existing, tense and defensive, caused time to slow way down. It showed Jaye just how incredibly long his sentence was going to be. There had to be some way to get sleep. He was dragging, nodding off during daylight hours from lying awake all night. The only hope he had was that Cash would be able to transfer him, like he'd said. Then, at least, Jaye would know what to expect. Maybe he could finally get some rest.

"Let's go, ladies!" the guard yelled, knocking against the cement block wall with his baton.

The last few guys lingering under the hot spray of the shower heads hurried to finish rinsing off. The institutional soap they'd been given was green and greasy, and no matter how hard you tried to scrub it off again, it left a slick film behind. Jaye had already dried off, using the towel to rub away the residue, and was waiting by the door to be allowed to leave.

He didn't like the showers. There was a row of sinks, and a large open area in which everyone showered together, with blue tiles on the walls and floor, and drains here and there. A few slim windows with bars let in some daylight, but, like with the rest of the prison, it was the fluorescents that did most of the work. He tried not to look too closely at the drains in the floor and sinks, because when he did, he sometimes saw a few spiders and cockroaches skittering out. After growing up in a less than ideal apartment, and his mother busy with other things on her mind than cleaning, he was used to pests to some extent. It didn't mean he had to like it. Once he'd moved out on his own, with Kris, Jaye had taken over cleaning duties to avoid the bugs, vermin and filth. Being a clean person had always been a point of pride, so to be back somewhere infested made him feel distinctly uncomfortable and frantic.

Being in the showers meant dealing with an entirely different kind of pest. It made Jaye want to grow eyes in the back of his head. When he was standing, naked and wet, washing out his long hair or soaping up his body, he knew he was being watched, that the threat was real. He looked womanly compared to the other men. Cash had no pull over the new arrivals, though Jaye had appreciated the few times he heard Ro speak up to warn others off, so until they were mixed with the general population, anything was possible.

Jaye watched his ass and trusted no one.

The inmates lined up to return to the A & O area, wearing damp towels wrapping their mid-sections.

Finally, the guard began to lead them out of the showers. The long line shuffled forward. Jaye kept his eyes on the ground, trying to disappear. When he reached the doorway, a second guard stopped him abruptly, singling him out and blocking his way with a baton.

An upward glance showed him it was Dorrance, the creepy thirty-something guard who had happily watched Cash fuck Jaye bloody in the common area of Unit 4.

"Larson. Step aside," Dorrance said. The baton was stretched across the middle of Jaye's chest, halting his progress. With no other choice, Jaye knew he had to do as he was told. After a nod of Dorrance's head, Jaye moved over to let everyone else pass. It seemed since Jaye was called out, the other guys were picking up their pace a little, just so they didn't get called out too.

Henry caught Jaye's eye as he passed, but there was no way he could help. Maybe Jaye imagined it, but Henry seemed to apologize wordlessly, his expression concerned. Jaye returned the gaze, steadily, and then Henry was led around a corner and away with everyone else.

The first guard had supervised the procession of inmates back to their cell. Jaye didn't make eye contact with Dorrance. He just waited, bracing himself.

"Okay, go ahead in," Dorrance said. At first Jaye was confused, and didn't understand the command. Then he saw there was someone behind the guard, in the hall.

It was Cash.

Cash circled the guard and took hold of Jaye by the arm, leading him back into the bathroom, now empty except for the two of them. Jaye wasn't sure if he was relieved or not.

Chapter 8
Fair Trade

It had been four days since he'd seen Cash, and he'd been a little afraid the deal wasn't going to happen after all; that their whole discussion in Unit 4 had just been an excuse to fuck the girly new kid. The evidence that the deal might still be on was encouraging; the anticipation of what Cash might be about to do to him was not.

Dorrance moved into the shower's doorway, blocking access from the hall, but facing Cash and Jaye. With a cold shiver racing down his spine, Jaye figured it was so the corrupt guard could watch the show again.

Jaye's hair was dripping, the drops dampening the towel where it hugged his ass. He caught glimpses of his and Cash's reflections in the mirrors above the sink, and he couldn't help but compare. Cash easily had twice the size and muscle mass of Jaye. He was a man, where Jaye was a boy. They both had tattoos, though Cash had many more. Jaye's bird wrapped his chest, shoulder, the right side of his neck and his back, embracing him but providing only imaginary comfort. The tribal tattoo above his cock was mostly concealed by the towel. Jaye had shaved before he'd showered, so his jaw was smooth, not that shaving made much of a difference anyway. Jaye's facial hair didn't come in fast or thick.

Cash's elbows were wrapped with inked cobwebs and blue-grey spiders skittered down his arms. The branded numbers on his neck kept catching Jaye's eye. It was impossible to deny that the scars slashing down through Cash's face and the facial tattoos made him look scary and intimidating. The cool color of his eyes held no warmth and the hard set of his mouth, the clench of his jaw as he bit down on his back teeth, only added to the overwhelming impression of being faced with a heartless, headstrong thug.

"You think I forgot about you, Johnny?" Cash smirked. He ran the back of his index finger down over the bluejay wing's feathers etched on Jaye's chest.

"Yeah, I was gettin' there. The deal's still on, right?"

Cash's finger stroked Jaye's nipple, then paused to tug on it. A flare of shameful stimulation and queasiness rippled outward from that small point of contact.

"It's been a few days," Cash allowed, his gaze slipping and sliding all over Jaye's half-naked body. Cash's finger hooked in the edge of the towel by Jaye's hip and tugged hard on it. The towel came loose, and Jaye let it fall to the floor, even though instinct made him want to grab it before he was exposed.

Swallowing thickly, he glanced at Dorrance in the doorway. Dorrance was halfway watching the hall and halfway watching Jaye's naked body with a hungry expression that left Jaye feeling uneasy and panicked.

Cash stroked down over the tribal tattoo to Jaye's flaccid cock. Jaye was way too nervous to get aroused, and that was bad. He knew he had to mentally overcome the fear and force himself to get interested, fast. Sensing that Cash could see Jaye's inner struggle didn't help him succeed. The more Jaye failed to get hard and calm down, the more jittery and afraid he became.

Playing with Jaye's dick like he didn't care how stiff it was, Cash said, "After popping that cherry, I figured I'd let your little ass heal up before fuckin' it wide open again. You bleeding?"

"N-no. Not anymore." Jaye was a little stunned to hear Cash had waited simply to let him recover. It helped ease him into more of a feeling of control, even if he was bare-assed naked in a prison bathroom with a thug and a dirty guard.

Cash reached for the waistband of his pants. Before he could even pull them down, Jaye was already getting down on his knees at Cash's feet. The eagerness made Cash chuckle — a vibration of sound amplified by the bathroom's acoustics. Jaye barely had a glimpse of Cash's shockingly thick cock before he was licking it with the flat of his tongue, pressing it up with his hand, then catching the head with his lips and taking it in over his tongue.

"Guess you *have* done this before," Cash sighed with pleasure. "Thought maybe you were just a desperate straight kid. Wouldn't be the first."

Jaye tried to tune it all out — where they were, that they were being watched, that they could get caught at any moment, and that Cash could turn out to be a lot crueler than he seemed. All that mattered was the warm cock stretching Jaye's jaws wide open and sliding on his tongue, leaving a salty trail over his taste buds. It was a lot thicker than any dick Jaye had personally encountered before, though the length was average in size. That had to have been why the sex had hurt so much, and why he'd torn enough to bleed. When Jaye took most of Cash's dick into his mouth, it stretched him open so wide, completely filling his throat, his jaw started to ache.

Cash held Jaye by his damp hair, guiding his speed. He eased Jaye forward and back, pumping his hips as he rode Jaye's mouth. Other than the ache in his jaw, there was no real pain, and it was all pretty familiar. Jaye started to actually enjoy himself a little, despite the cold tiles grinding against his knees, the damp, chilly air pebbling his flesh, and the overall disturbing feeling he had because of Dorrance.

The wet sucking, slurping sounds were louder than they should have been, making the act feel more obscene than it was. The natural taste of Cash's dick and his pre-come slicked Jaye's tongue. Jaye let himself enjoy the flavor, since it was going to be keeping him alive for the foreseeable future. The more he worshipped that thick cock, the more likely he was to keep breathing.

When Cash eased Jaye back far enough to pull out, his fat dick sliding in a wet trail over Jaye's flushed-hot, throbbing lips, Jaye was actually a little disappointed.

Cash held Jaye by the chin, tilting his face up, and said with a half-closed, thoughtful stare, "You're pretty, like a girl. If it wasn't for that dick hanging between your legs...."

Jaye lowered his gaze submissively. "That's why I need you."

"You might want to, but you're not cutting your hair. Not one inch. I like it the way it is."

"No problem."

"Stand up," Cash ordered. Once Jaye was on his feet, Cash added,

"Turn around. Bend over."

Dorrance loudly cleared his throat, like he wanted to remind Jaye he was there, enjoying every second of his humiliation. Jaye could feel Dorrance's stare as though it was a physical touch sliding over his skin. He grabbed hold of the nearest sink and stuck out his ass, arching his back and widening his stance a little.

When he felt the first touch of blunt pressure at his hole, Jaye couldn't help but grimace, anticipating pain. Cash was watching Jaye in the mirror and grinning a little in clear amusement. With his hands, he spread Jaye's cheeks to nestle between them, then slowly pushed to enter. He went so slow, the burn of the stretch was only intensified. It took forever for the bulbous head to pass through his rim. Struggling to bear it, Jaye grunted, loudly, and winced, but tried not to clench. He blew out a breath and closed his eyes.

When the head finally eased through the narrowest part of his sphincter, Jaye shuddered, moaning softly. Panting through his nostrils, he clawed at the sink's smooth, cool porcelain, all of his attention on the stiff cock spreading him out impossibly wide. It felt like Cash was wearing him, and any slight movement would tear Jaye apart.

"Bet you wish I had a smaller dick," Cash chuckled, pushing to burrow deeper and simultaneously pulling Jaye back onto him. Whimpering at the continued stretch moving farther into his body, Jaye's eyebrows tilted in a plaintive expression. Just like the first time, it felt like he had the wrong end of a baseball bat stuck up in there. It felt wrong and torturous, especially being displayed as he was. There was no privacy, nothing sacred or sweet about it.

In the mirror's reflection, Cash gazed contentedly down at the sight of Jaye's ass taking his cock. Jaye's cheeks were spread so Cash could see more of his hole gripping the dark red shaft. He hummed happily, rubbing Jaye's rim, and bottomed out. Kneading Jaye's cheeks, Cash said, "I'm no faggot, but I've got twenty years in this fuckin' place. Ain't no pussy in here, just ass. I figure, I fuck the guy who looks like a fifteen year old girl, and it doesn't make a difference that you've got balls. You take cock before?"

"Twice," Jaye rasped, his lips quivering on a gasp, unable to think past the throbbing, aching stretch.

Cash chuckled. Holding Jaye's hips, he slowly tugged back out, watching Jaye's body expel the shaft. Then, just as slowly, Cash pressed right back in, pulling Jaye back onto him. Jaye let out a shaky exhale through parted lips, but bit back a hard whimper.

"Just means I've gotta train you to take it easier. Huh?"

"Yes, sir," he growled as he took the next thrust.

"How old are you, boy?"

"Nineteen."

"Your dick ain't hard. Is that because of how much this hurts right now, or because of me?"

Jaye wasn't sure what the best answer to that was. The truth was it was neither of those things, but was being honest worse?

"Scared," he murmured.

"Ain't nothing here to be scared of. Anything scares you, I take care of it, got it? Anything else?"

"I'm a... embarrassed. By being watched."

Cash chuckled and pushed hard, their bodies as joined as they could possibly be. He slapped the side of Jaye's ass and held him still.

"Gotta teach you to get over that, too, 'cause I like to show off my things, especially if letting my friends watch my bitch get butt-fucked earns me favors. Got it?"

"Got it," Jaye grunted, his eyes downcast.

Jaye intentionally clenched up on the cock and rolled his hips a little. He let his hand fall between his legs to tug at his dick. He caught Cash watching like he approved, so he kept going. "I'll make it real good for you," Jaye promised.

Cash kept taking it easy on him, going slow and gentle. He caressed up Jaye's spine to grab the back of his neck, grinding against his tightly clenched cheeks. Jaye sighed, frowning, and jacked his cock faster. The fingers wrapping the back of his neck gripped hard enough to bruise and he arched, fully hard, his balls beginning to draw up.

"That's it," Cash praised. "You like that?"

"Fuck yes," Jaye moaned.

"What do you like about it?"

Feeling Dorrance's stare, Jaye closed his eyes, stroked himself and focused on the thick cock up his ass. "I like how you fuck me. The feel of your huge cock stuffed up my ass. I like feeling like I'm yours, and no one else's."

"Good." Cash caressed the scar on Jaye's back. "This new?"

Jaye nodded. "They tried to gut me, so I cut that fucker's throat and stabbed the other one. That's why I'm in here."

"Fuck, Johnny. You're a tougher little shit than I thought," Cash laughed.

"No one hurts me like that again."

"You a fighter?"

They locked eyes in the mirror, Cash still giving it slow and easy, Jaye getting closer to climax, getting off on the tenderness.

"I can be."

"Any time I fuck you around other guys, you fight a little. Got it? Make it look good, like this dick is fuckin' tearing you up instead of making you wet. But when it's just you and me, I expect to see how much you wanna take this cock. You show me you need it, every time."

"Got it," Jaye managed a tight smile. "No problem."

Cash thrust all the way in and held there. He guided Jaye upright, to rest back against Cash's chest. Then, he reached around for Jaye's cock, and let it slide through his loosely curled fingers. After a few strokes, Jaye pulsed tiny beads of fluid, slicking Cash's fingers.

"You see my friend down there?" He nodded in Dorrance's direction. Jaye grunted in assent. Dorrance had his arms folded over his chest, his gaze fixed on Cash's hand stroking Jaye's stiffened dick. "He's doing us a big favor, getting you moved in with me real soon. You know what happens when someone does you a favor, right?"

"You've gotta pay them back," Jaye answered, the dread sinking in and pulling him down. Like he could feel Jaye's interest wilting, Cash squeezed tighter and fondled him more brazenly, gripping around Jaye's pink crown and rubbing over the tip with his thumb.

"That's right," Cash sighed, grinding shallowly into Jaye's ass.

"I gotta fuck him or something?" Jaye asked, hating the idea with pure, dripping venom.

"Mmm, not as simple as that. He's got a friend who makes pornos. Remember how I said you're gonna act like you're fighting back with me, when we've got company? Well, you're gonna fight back when the time is right, for my friend. We'll go someplace private. Take some video. Make it look *rough*." He gave the end of Jaye's dick a tighter squeeze, making him moan in discomfort. "It pays the debt."

"One time deal?"

"One time deal," Cash agreed. He bent Jaye over again, but kept jacking him with complete strokes. Jaye tipped up his ass, inviting each thrust. They came faster, and a little harder. The pain was long gone and it only felt good. Frowning against the rough pushes jolting him forward, Jaye circled his hips to ride Cash's hand and moaned more loudly. "But this? This is every fuckin' day. And as you can see, I don't mind you showing my friend what a cock slut you really are. He's the only exception."

Jaye let out a breathy cry as his climax hit. He spurted over Cash's fingers and the sink. Shivering with pleasure, Jaye watched as Cash shook Jaye's dick, spraying the drops. From the corner of his eye, he saw Dorrance in the doorway, palming his crotch like he was playing with himself.

Jaye's ass tensed with orgasm. Cash growled and rode him for a few more moments, then pulled out. Suddenly astonishingly empty, Jaye felt hot semen splash over his lower back and his sore, fucked-out ass.

Cash stroked through the spend with two fingers, rubbing it through Jaye's ass crack. Then he pushed both fingers through Jaye's pucker to smear his seed inside as well. Breathing hard, flushed and twisted up with both an unlikely, proud joy and shame at what a whore he knew he'd suddenly become, Jaye held Cash's stare in the mirror. Telling himself to turn on the charm, Jaye moaned, begging, "*More.*"

Chapter 9
Devilish Whispers

The walk from the A & O area to their assigned Housing Units was unnerving. Jaye felt little twinges in his side with each step, as if his memories of the attack were trying to undermine his attempts to move on and keep going. Limping slightly, he walked down the halls with his bedroll, toiletries, and the rest of his few, meager possessions, feeling eyes on him the whole time. Every step was controlled and orchestrated by FCI. Several guards ushered them along, dividing the group, then leading each to the various Housing Units once they reached the central nexus of the prison. When they approached or passed a section or room containing inmates, everyone inside stopped what they were doing, staring at the newcomers. It made him feel like a mouse entering an overcrowded lion's den. He was powerless and utterly without privacy.

As Jaye walked into Unit 4 with a fraction of the other new arrivals, including Ro, he was perplexed to find there were no cat calls until he passed by some of the black inmates. It was kind of fascinating. The white and Latino guys didn't say a word. That hadn't been the case before, when he'd gone to find Cash. In Anchorage, in the neighborhood where he'd lived and grown up, there was much less ethnic diversity than there seemed to be in Oregon. But there had been a good enough mix in Anchorage that Jaye had always known not to categorize people based on appearances. He'd felt the anti-gay sentiment from many people in his life — teachers, friends, the parents of friends, neighbors, shop keeps — ever since he was a kid, realizing he was queer. It wasn't always spoken. Sometimes the hatred was simply in the way the energy of some people came rushing at you, and had nothing to do with their heritage. It was just them.

If someone with that hatred inside them entered prison, he imagined it translated in unique ways. He was sure their loathing of gay men didn't vanish, but did it make them want to get violent and use their fists to make their point? Or did they prefer to take something else in hand to send a message of dominance over someone they'd prejudged as being weaker?

Certainly Jaye's natural enjoyment of sex with men made him a specific type of target, luring in the hard-up men locked away for years on end. He was prey, but his proclivities and talents had also won him Cash. But maybe some of these men just wanted to hurt him for being so willing to give up his ass and mouth, and they'd try to come at him with homemade weapons, or just their bare hands and rage.

He had seen already, even with how segregated they kept the new arrivals, that most of the gangs formed around skin tone. And suddenly, everyone seemed to be backing off except the black guys. It was both weirdly reassuring to have at least some people seem to accept him, and scary to know exactly who his enemies were.

"Hey, sweet cheeks! C'mere! C'mere, baby!"

He kept his head down, the limp getting worse as he felt an immaterial blade split his skin and sink into the muscles of his abdomen. *Gonna slice open your belly. Pull your insides out. Make you watch.*

The more he focused to shut out the catcalls around him and the taunting inside his head, the more tunnel vision Jaye experienced. He ignored almost everything except where he was walking.

The female guard pointed at a cell. Her lips moved but no sound came out, as far as he could tell. Or, maybe his mental noise was drowning it out. Jaye kept moving, walking to where she'd pointed, moving through the doorway and leaving most of the prison behind.

The smaller space felt like a cocoon and helped him catch his breath. The phantom pressure in his side was making it hard to draw in air. He set down his things on the empty, stripped bottom bunk and pressed a hand against his scar. There was a small desk behind him, a small locker for each of the cell's occupant's personal possessions, the toilet and sink, and a tiny window. One of the lockers had a small framed photograph of a middle-aged woman set on top of it, beside a wooden cross set on a stand. The cell's door shut with a bang and locked. Cash used the step to come down from the top bunk and said nothing. He just eyed the guard as she trapped them both inside the small space together.

Jaye heard the latch catch, felt the space around him diminish even more, shrinking steadily like some magic trick. The walls drew in. His body felt too large, heavy, and cumbersome. Like when he was chasing Earl with the knife, his body had pulled him down.

He still couldn't breathe. His lungs refused to expand. The urge to lash out and expend the crazy, frantic energy was strong. Starting to get lightheaded, he crouched down where he was and held his head in his hands, his hair pooling on the concrete.

"You're okay. You're okay," he muttered to himself. "They're not here. You're okay."

Everything that made him panic was bubbling up.

Kris doesn't care. He ditched me, vanishing when I needed him most and abandoned me. I could have died and he didn't give a shit.

Mom never showed. Is she dead? Did she finally just OD? Did one of her client's kill her and dump the body like they were gonna dump mine?

Do I have the strength to survive this? To fight every day just to stay alive, when there are people actively trying to hurt or kill me? Maybe it's better to give up, admit defeat. I could just kill myself. It'd be less painful than any other way this could go.

"Stand up. Come on. Up."

It was Cash. He sounded so determined, so strong, like he was made of stone instead of flesh and didn't even know what it was like to be scared.

Jaye did stand, though he didn't want to. He turned to face his cellmate.

Cash stared him down, stepping forward, into Jaye's personal space. Jaye's breathing was rough and uneven. The panic kept growing, overwhelming him.

Is he going to ask me to suck him off right here? Right now?

Can I do this? I can't do this. I don't know this guy. I don't want to have to rely on him when everyone else has always failed me.

The closer Cash got, the more the panic took over. Jaye pushed at Cash's chest, his arms shooting out defensively. Cash just caught

Jaye's wrists. Jaye kept struggling and fighting with everything he had, planting his feet for leverage, using his shoulders, grunting with effort, but Cash wasn't moved an inch. He didn't even have to try.

If I ever do need to fight him off of me, I'll never be able to manage it. I'll always be helpless with him.

Wheezing, suffocating, Jaye heard dimly, "Look at where you are. This is yours now. Your space. Look at it. Ain't no one getting in."

"I can't do this," Jaye panted, still fighting, but less now. He was giving in to the hopelessness.

"*Look!*"

The volume of the command got him to do it. He looked again around the cell. It was small, but he could see the whole thing. There were no places to hide.

"Before, they all yelled things at me," Jaye told Cash. "The guys out there. Not this time. This time, when I walked in here, it was just—"

"The blacks. Not all, but most. They're the Warlords," Cash finished. "Rivals of ours. That's just how it is in here. Got nothing to do with you, Johnny. No one fucking touches you. My crew and I will handle the others. I'm the commander of the Disciples in FCI Sheridan. I call the fucking shots."

"Okay," Jaye nodded, calming down a little.

"We're a fucking institution, you know that, right? This ain't just local shit. The Disciples are a goddamned nationwide organization. When we need to flex a little muscle, it's nothin' to us to grab those motherfuckers by the throat and squeeze. You heard how my guys shut their fucking mouths? You know why that is?"

Jaye nodded. "You."

"Damn fucking right."

"Okay," Jaye repeated, calming down almost completely. He stopped fighting. Cash let him go. "Sorry," Jaye said with embarrassment. "Thanks. I swear I'm not always this much of a pussy. Things have just been a lot to take lately. Like you. But the more I do it, the easier it'll be, right?"

"Right," Cash grinned. "You know, I like you, kid. I think this is gonna work out just fine."

Chapter 10
The New Normal

Every minute Jaye had been conscious since the attack had felt like an endless whirl of real and imagined bad things, until he was moved to his cell with Cash. Only then did things start to fall into a recognizable order. From the very first day, Jaye found himself floating off in his head much less frequently than he had before. He stayed anchored in reality instead of functioning on a base animal response level of constantly being ready to fuck, fight, or die. Of course, there was still plenty of that at the edge of things, but other priorities began to shift in his orbit, like exercise or hunger. Most of all, he had a strong desire to get a firm grasp on everything around him or anything he was responsible for.

Resting on his cot, the bed tightly made, military style, according to House Rules and Regulations, Jaye enjoyed his incredibly limited view of the outer corridor of the prison. Beyond the walkway just outside the locked door, through the narrow, unbreakable window, he could see some of the common area and a couple of cells on the opposite side of Unit 4. There was some movement out there as a few inmates were led away to their work assignments by a guard. It was all controlled. Orderly. Locked down. He liked that he could see most of his cell without even needing to turn his head. It was comforting that he didn't need to worry about anyone sneaking up behind him. He could see when a guard walked by, and could tell by the way the light changed when the sun was shifting behind a cloud way up in the sky somewhere. He also always noticed when Cash got up and exactly what he did when he was moving around their cell. All of the information he needed to feel safe was right there in front of him.

There had been so much sprung on him without warning, or ripped away permanently in a short amount of time—the job he'd worked for years to attain and earn, his less than ideal but no less important relationship with his boyfriend, his cherished apartment, his ability to check in on and take care of his mom, and his health—the impulse to gather close what he *did* have left and guard it fiercely was very strong.

He had a small collection of necessities for grooming—shaving supplies, a hairbrush, deodorant, toothpaste, toothbrush, soap and towels. All of these basics had been given to him without charge because he was indigent, every penny of the small amount of money he'd had in his bank account had gone to medical and legal costs. If he needed to restock, he had been told he could get items on credit until he was able to begin his own work assignment and start earning money for the commissary. Looking good for Cash had suddenly became one of Jaye's biggest responsibilities, so he was relieved to know he would be able to take care of himself.

He had a book about basic mechanics borrowed from the prison library. One of the A & O lectures had explained the work assignments and apprenticeship programs at FCI Sheridan. Right away Jaye had latched on to the idea of joining Mechanical Services, which was responsible for maintenance, utilities, and new construction at the facility. It was a better, more practical trade to learn than low-level retail management. If he stuck with it, he could gain training and experience with plumbing, welding, the machine shop, electrical, air conditioning or landscaping details. Any of those options seemed like a good way to get on the path to employment following his release.

He had his cot, his cell, and his cellmate. The small locker he was allotted in their unit was mostly empty, apart from some paperwork gathered during orientation. There had been so much crap he'd carted from his mom's apartment over to the one he moved into with Kris. Boxes and boxes of old mementos, photographs, clothes, shoes, or just *stuff* that didn't fall into any category had been painstakingly hefted out of one place and into another just to sit in the spare closet in a stack of both his and Kris's unopened moving boxes.

He figured all of that was gone now, tossed in a dumpster somewhere, just like Burt and Earl had almost tossed him, or like some other monster had likely tossed Cora. Kris had probably sold what he could and tossed the rest himself.

Did he get a chill, when he swung the bags into the metal bin? Did he realize how close I'd been to being a carved-out body lying on trash bags? Did he even care?

The more Jaye focused on the idea of that, Kris standing in the same alley Jaye had nearly died in, treating all Jaye had left in the world like worthless shit, the more plausible it became.

If he couldn't even be bothered to write, or text more than two short words, what use was there in being respectful of my possessions?

Sometimes it made Jaye angry. But, slowly, Jaye was learning to be glad he didn't have any of that to worry about anymore. It was no longer his problem. Hell, he couldn't even bring himself to worry if his mom was alive, because there was simply nothing he could do about it. He'd tried calling her. His calls were never answered or returned. Sure, at first he'd worried, but there was better use for his energy, especially when his own wellbeing was in so much jeopardy. All of his previous mental preoccupations had been put on hold, frozen in place until he was able to rejoin the world.

The more days passed with everything pretty much the same as the ones before them, the more confident Jaye became. Having a clear idea of what he needed to do and not do, adhering to a specifically delineated, mandatory schedule, kept him going and gave him some peace.

One of the female guards walked past, from right to left. Her footsteps receded perfectly down the walkway, all the way to the end. Each step was distinct, crisp. They faded away at a specifically measured pace. The fullness of each of those sounds underscored the enormity and cold rigidity of the prison interior. It was impossible for him to get claustrophobic when the space just beyond his cell was so big.

Those were the things he liked. He also liked the way the water sounded as it rushed through the pipes around them, in the walls. That sense of fluid movement was a great reminder time sped onward every second, constantly draining away the total amount left on his sentence.

The rush of water also let his mind whisk away, past the boundaries of his cell, whooshing to every part of the building, then out into the wide world.

Dinnertime arrived. That meant it was time to venture out of his oasis and back into dangerous territory. He could get food, or choose to go to the exercise yard instead. The guards had them file along in a Controlled Movement to the cafeteria style dining hall where they automatically lined up in an equally orderly way for their trays of food. Jaye was always near Cash in the food line, which set Jaye's mind at ease. It seemed everyone else stayed away from Cash out of fear or respect, but so far Cash had come through for Jaye.

They stood there, shuffling a step forward every few moments, waiting to grab a plastic orange tray pre-loaded with the day's offerings, handed over by inmates who worked in Food Services. That evening they were serving chicken chow mein with chicken gravy, green beans, white rice, peas and carrots, three slices of bread, two squares of margarine, a fresh apple and an unnaturally red fruit punch drink.

The food didn't smell particularly appetizing, but the variety of things on the tray would at least increase his odds of being able to stomach some of it.

He didn't like how many people were in the room with him, and the close quarters of the food queue. There were so many voices echoing off the cement walls and linoleum floors. Jaye tried to tune out whatever was being said around him. It was better to mind his own business and keep his head down, whether they were talking about him or not. No one usually smiled at him, or did anything kind, but if they did, it only made him more defensive.

The first day after he'd moved in with Cash, waiting in line next to him, Jaye hadn't kept his head down. Instead, he'd noted the way others were looking between him and Cash, like assumptions were being made. Some of the guys smirked, gave him lecherous stares, or obscenely wriggled their tongue when he caught their eye.

Quickly, he figured out it was better to play dumb and not react to any of that. But sometimes he couldn't avoid noticing others' reactions. That evening, one of the Latino guys behind the food counter gave a little whistle as Jaye stepped up and reached for a tray, then looked up and down Jaye's body.

Right away, Cash spoke up, saying to the guy, "Shut your fucking mouth." It wasn't said aggressively, but calm and low.

The inmate cleared his throat and suddenly found the next tray of food very fascinating, because he wouldn't look up from it, even after they'd moved on and the next person reached for their food.

Jaye stayed quiet, but bit back a grin. Limping only slightly, his bad side aching less than it usually did, he followed Cash away from the food line and headed toward the long, metal tables with their bench seats.

The first time he'd been in the dining hall with Cash, Jaye had been profoundly nervous. His heart had been pounding. He hadn't wanted to do the wrong thing or assume he could sit at Cash's table, but if he belonged to Cash, he didn't know if he should sit with anyone else either. They hadn't talked about it before they'd left the cell. Cash wasn't much of an explainer, from what Jaye had seen. He just acted.

When they'd reached the table, things had been cleared up, fast.

Cash had slid his tray onto the table filled with the Disciples. Glancing back at Jaye from over his shoulder, Cash had said, in command, "You sit here." He pointed to the spot to his right.

It was the same that day, too.

"Hey boss! Looking good!" long-haired, easy-going Gravy said in greeting, raising an arm to wave as Cash got closer.

Jaye hung back slightly. The brown gravy on his tray sloshed around as he struggled to keep it steady.

Cash took an empty seat with plenty of space to his right. Once Cash was settled, that space was where Jaye sat down without looking up or speaking to anyone. His tray clattered against the tabletop. After he'd slid down onto his space on the bench, he pulled the tray close and hunched over it slightly, especially after one of the guys nearby began eying his apple like he wanted to take it.

Cash hadn't given Jaye specific requirements about avoiding eye contact with the guys on his crew, or said he preferred Jaye to remain silent and avoid conversation. But, at the moment, Jaye was still too much in survival mode to do anything but the bare necessities. Everyone was a threat. Every situation was deadly. That's why he knew he was still losing weight, the regulation clothing hanging off of him, his ribs protruding from his body more than they'd ever had as his fat reserves were eaten up.

Sitting next to Cash, eyes on his tray, not really eager to eat anything but palming his apple just to protect it, he was equal parts starving and nauseous. Jaye heard Cash ask his lieutenant, the second-in-command, Hax, "How's it going?"

"Going fine, boss. How's it going with you?" Hax handled a lot of the dirty work for the Disciples, from what Jaye could tell, or at least he was the one to delegate and organize the dirty work. He was pretty level-headed, in his late twenties and covered in tattoos from his knuckles to his chin, with a shaved head and bright blue eyes.

"No problems." Cash paused, giving Jaye the side-eye, like he was taking note of Jaye's shyness and reluctance to eat. A moment later, he gave another command. "Say hello to the guys, Johnny."

"Hello," Jaye murmured in his naturally raspy, soft voice, without looking up.

There was an awkward moment of silence, and Jaye used all of his strength to stay perfectly still, because he could feel all of the attention that was on him. It was deeply unsettling, just like it always was. They were all imagining it, he knew—Cash fucking him, Jaye acting the pathetic bitch to the real man at his side. Then, saving Jaye from further humiliation, Hax said, "Hey, boss, you heard about Ecker? Keeps tossing Kett's cell. Hasn't found anything, so—"

"Course he hasn't," Cash commented. With a sharp, upraised stare across the table at Hax, Cash took a bite of some colorless meat dripping with watery brown liquid.

"Yeah, we're not all as stupid as he is," Wolf laughed. Wolf was one of the crew Jaye liked the least. Wolf was big, bigger even than Cash, with a barrel chest and head-to-toe, thick body hair, and a mop of black hair on his head. Jaye got an unsettling vibe from Wolf, which started with how avidly he stared at Jaye's mouth and body when Cash wasn't looking. When Cash had fucked Jaye the first time, Wolf had been staring the whole time, practically with drool running down his chin. Sometimes, in the exercise yard, when the Disciples huddled in closer than the guards liked, Jaye would see Wolf with one of the really young inmates, pawing at them with a toothy grin on his face.

Outside of the prison, that kind of behavior almost certainly wouldn't fly with the crew, making Wolf a target for an attack. Child molesters and rapists were not tolerated. But inside the walls, all inmates were fair game, no matter their age. The rules changed when freedom was relinquished.

In response to Wolf's comment, Cash just raised an eyebrow and glanced over at Jaye.

Jaye finally glanced up, getting a quick view of how the left side of the table was watching him while acting like they weren't, before locking eyes with Cash.

"Eat," Cash said to Jaye. It sounded like an order.

Jaye's hands had been in his lap, cradling his apple, but he set that back down on the tray and moved to pick up his fork. The chatter along the table died down again as if each time Cash gave an order, they all stopped to listen in case one of the orders was directed at *them*. It was spooky enough to make Jaye obey.

Jaye tried some of the overcooked peas and carrots. There was no seasoning on them, and the taste had been boiled away, so they were an unappetizing lump of mush on his tongue. He did his best to choke them down. Once he'd swallowed, Cash stopped staring and went back to his conversation. The others started to loosen up and things settled into a sort of normalcy Jaye knew it was going to take him a long while to get used to.

Chapter 11
Prison Bitch Pays Up

The lights were out. The whole area was pretty quiet. Someone in a cell farther down the walkway started to yell, "You don't get to fucking touch my book!" The guard yelled over them to shut the hell up, that it was their one and only warning. There were footsteps, whispering, and movement, but it was a low hum of activity, punctuated only by small, temporary bangs, distant buzzing and other atmospheric noise.

In the dark, Cash climbed down from his bunk and got on top of Jaye, who had been lying on his back. It wasn't unexpected, but right away, Jaye's anxiety started to churn. Whether he liked it or not, it was time to perform and compensate Cash for his trouble by letting him do whatever he wanted to Jaye's body. Jaye's breathing and heart rate sped up as Cash settled between his legs, nudging them apart. Jaye could feel Cash's body heat warming him and smelled the scent of mint toothpaste on his breath. There was just enough light to show Jaye the eager gleam to his owner's pale eyes.

"Pants down," Cash ordered.

Nervously, Jaye obeyed, sliding the pants down past his hips. Taking his underwear with them, he pushed them as low as he could in the position he was in. Then, he curled his legs up to get the clothes the rest of the way off. After he was naked from the waist down, and feeling a little horrified about it, since they didn't have privacy and never would, Jaye let his legs come down again, on either side of Cash. Being spread that much made it next to impossible to relax or calm down.

Cash pushed Jaye's shirt up to expose his chest and stomach, then traced the knife wound on Jaye's side. "The guys who did this. They fuck with you?" he asked quietly.

"Yeah, in a few different ways. Dragged me out of bed, tried to knock me out, chased me down, pinned, stripped, and fingered me 'til I fought back. Killed that motherfucker with his own knife."

"No shit?" Cash commented, looking a little impressed. He folded his hand around Jaye's dick and began to play with it. The light, exploratory touches made it even harder to breathe normally, some of Jaye's fight instincts kicking in. He grabbed handfuls of the blanket beneath him. Shivers chased up from his balls into his gut, then went down his legs. Reflexively, Jaye wanted to wrestle Cash off of him, but he couldn't do that. Even if he got out from under Cash, where would Jaye go? They were locked in together, and any sign that he wasn't cooperating might cost him the deal keeping him in one piece.

It was completely unlike the way Kris had touched Jaye, and was slightly, disturbingly similar to the ways Burt had touched him. Jaye fought to override his reflexes and be still, but it all just transformed into tension in his body, like he was a rubber band, pulled tight and ready to snap. "Guess you're not as much of a pussy as I thought. You're a little badass, aren't you?"

Not a badass right now, Jaye thought, not letting the grimace show on his face as Cash pulled gently on the end of Jaye's dick.

"I should give you a tear for that. Like mine. Shows people not to fuck with you."

Fuck with me like you are, Cash? They'll always fuck with me, you know that. Nothing fixes what's wrong with me, especially not one little facial tattoo.

Eerily, like he could read Jaye's thoughts, Cash said, "Might seem like just a little mark, little bit of ink, but in here it's good to give people reasons to be afraid of you. You've got a tear, means you've killed, and you could do it again."

"Yeah," Jaye replied, more shakily than he'd have liked. Cash's hand rubbed down over the wrinkled skin of Jaye's balls. Gathering them up in his hand, he brushed his thumb back and forth, tickling a little.

Jaye was confused by the foreplay, since Cash had already said he wasn't gay, but Jaye knew he had no room to question or complain. Cash had every right to do anything he wanted. He'd paid for it a few

74

times over already. But, it did make it weirder to be enjoying sex that was essentially a business transaction.

"Spread your legs. Wide as you can. Relax."

Self-consciously, Jaye did as asked, letting his knees fall open completely. To have his most vulnerable areas at the mercy of a frightening stranger was overwhelming, so Jaye let his head fall back to rest on the pillow and worked to calm down. He had to force himself to trust Cash to want to protect his property.

"I'm a scary guy, aren't I?" Cash said with a faint grin. "Does it scare you to have me playing around down here?"

He pulled on Jaye's sac in a way that was more uncomfortable than painful, causing Jaye to grunt and blush. Tipping his chin up, he closed his eyes and tried not to frown.

Is it better to make Cash think he's scary, or not? Is it better to build up Cash's ego or try to make myself seem like less of a pussy?

Jaye couldn't think around it, not when he had such a powerful man pulling on his scrotum. The skin stretched out the more Cash pulled on Jaye's balls. Jaye made a breathy sound through parted lips before he could think to self-censor.

He decided, hastily, that Cash already knew Jaye was pussy enough to give up his ass, so he really didn't have much to lose in going that route.

"A little. Don't know you well yet, and you're a lot bigger than me," he answered.

"Mm," Cash hummed, nodding. Jaye didn't know if that was good or bad. He pressed Jaye's balls back against his crotch, rolling them. Then he gathered up Jaye's softened cock, closed his fingers around it and gave it a firm tug, letting the pink head peek out the end of his fist.

"You wanna know how this is gonna go?"

"Please," Jaye replied. His knees quivered as Cash brushed the tip of his thumb over Jaye's slit, playing with it and stimulating sensitive nerve endings.

"Okay. I fuck you, maybe play around down here, too, every night, and whenever else I want. You suck my dick every morning, and whenever else I tell you to. Got it?"

"Got it," Jaye answered breathlessly as Cash squeezed around his crown firmly enough to make Jaye

writhe, his breathing getting heavier. The ways Cash was touching him were starting to make Jaye hard. Cash was more of a man than anyone Jaye had ever met before in his life. Looks aside, since Jaye wasn't physically attracted to Cash very much at all, it was hot to have someone so powerful giving him focused, relatively gentle attention.

Cash relaxed his grip, then squeezed again. Jaye's hips twitched, thrusting helplessly into Cash's hand. Pre-ejaculate dampened his tip.

"You like that?" Cash asked. He rubbed through the wetness. Seeing it, Jaye swelled and stiffened. Cash continued his squeeze, release, rub, squeeze, release motions.

"Yeah," Jaye admitted.

"Then say thank you."

"Thank you," Jaye breathed, pushing a little into Cash's hand. Cash's free hand came up to cup the side of Jaye's jaw, and his thumb rubbed over Jaye's parted, gasping lips.

"You're gonna be hard when I fuck your ass, right? Show me how hot you are to take my cock?"

"Mm-hmm," Jaye grunted, pushing a little harder, biting on his lower lip.

"No, don't be fucking silent. Tell me what you want."

Jaye's fear notched up and he felt a cold sweat breaking out on his body. "P-please fuck me. Want you to. I love taking your cock."

"Show me."

A fresh, hard shiver raced down Jaye's spine, and it was all terror.

"Legs back. Come on."

He curled them up toward his chest, holding his hands under his knees. He hated the position, how open and vulnerable it left him. Cash could see everything—how hard Jaye's dick was, his balls, his hole, even his face.

Cash sucked on his index finger, then twisted it through Jaye's hole. It bent as it went in, rubbing against his passage.

"That's nice. See how your dick jumps when I do that? Like it's begging? Means you like it. What do we say?"

"Thank you," Jaye breathed, clenching reflexively on the finger, staring at it pushing further into his ass, twisting around in there. "I do like it."

His heart was pounding, and the desire to cry was right near the surface.

Cash pulled the finger out, rubbed over Jaye's hole, prying at it. The finger plunged in fast, to the last knuckle as Cash sighed. "After we do my friend his favor, show him a little role-play for his porn buddies, we'll have access to lube, okay?"

"O-okay," Jaye stuttered.

Cash watched Jaye's hole taking the pumping finger. It was rubbing at him in there in a way that made Jaye's toes curl. His dick was still getting harder, too, jutting up against his belly, straight and red. Cash could see all of that, all the humiliation.

"Spread that ass. Use your hands. Go on. You're my bitch, right? So show me."

Jaye grabbed his cheeks and pulled them apart, trembling a little, feeling like he was doing an awful job at manning up.

Hooking the tip of his finger in Jaye's hole to pull it open, Cash spat a thick wad of saliva right down into it, then pushed the fluid in with a second finger.

Jaye growled a little at the small, intimate ache, but bore it, his jaw clenched. For a few minutes, it was just Cash leisurely fingering Jaye's ass and watching him get really hard. Few things had ever made Jaye as ashamed of his sexual orientation as that moment, even though, logically, he knew it was also saving his life.

Inspiration struck as Cash pulled the fingers out and spat again into Jaye's hole, so Jaye said, "Thank you for the prep."

"You're welcome," Cash said with a hungry grin, pushing three fingers through Jaye's throbbing, oversensitive rim. "Gotta safeguard my property, don't I? Never seen a guy get so hard for dick before. They're usually limp as a noodle. You really like the feel of those fingers up there, huh?"

"Yeah, feels nice," Jaye grunted, flushed red with shame. All of those nights with Kris, begging him for sex, they had caught up to him. Jaye did like that Cash wanted to fuck him. It was something Jaye had been yearning for throughout their relationship, though he never pictured his wish being granted in a prison cell with someone like Cash.

"You've been very cooperative so far," Cash commented, twisting his hand around inside Jaye's anal passage and pressing in hard enough to hurt, especially when his fingers spread out widely. Jaye made a frowning whimper and flexed his feet, knowing he wasn't allowed to complain. He needed to find ways to cope silently if it started to become painful.

"Whenever you want me to suck or fuck you, let you in my pants, I'll be ready. Rather be ready than dead."

"Good motto, kid," Cash smiled. He tugged his hand out, shifted higher and pulled out his cock. He spat in his palm and spread the saliva on his dick. It was almost as big around as Jaye's wrist. Cash aligned the head with Jaye's hole.

Jaye couldn't help the tense whimper he made as he watched Cash begin to enter him. As the broad crown pressed slowly through his rim, stretching it out to its limit, Jaye swallowed a sharp cry, biting down on his cheek. His whole body convulsed a little in outrage at the sensation of being penetrated by something so thick. Gripping his ass, shaking and sweating, Jaye breathed heavily through his nose and felt his head spin.

"That's it," Cash sighed. "That's nice."

The head popped through. Jaye had been curled up a little with tension, folded in half and leaning forward, but collapsed then in relief, just trying to adjust and cope. His head rolled to the side, resting on the pillow as Cash grabbed hold of Jaye's deflating dick and began to pump it while he sheathed himself deeper.

He knew he was wincing, even while bearing down onto Cash's thickness, just wanting to have it over with. He tried to find some pleasure too. He had no choice.

When Cash was fully sheathed, with Jaye impaled and folded up underneath him, Cash relaxed more completely on top of him, with Jaye's legs resting on Cash's shoulders. There was just enough space between them for Cash's hand to keeping toying with Jaye's dick.

His fingers gently smeared precious amounts of sticky fluid over the shaft as pain melted into enjoyment, all on its own.

"You like that?" Cash chuckled.

"Yeah," Jaye frowned, grimacing more as Cash thrust, moving shallowly and still stroking. After a few more thrusts, Jaye moaned softly. The sound seemed to turn Cash on, because his thrusts got faster, though not harder. He just worked Jaye steadily until Jaye was coming with a harder moan, shooting over his own stomach as Cash shook the drops off Jaye's dick.

After Jaye was spent, he went lax, just letting Cash fuck him, laying there wide open and taking it easily. It went on for a while, with Cash frowning in concentration, mouth open and gasping.

Before he unloaded, Cash pulled out and came over Jaye's tipped-up ass. Warm drips slipped down through Jaye's crack and over his cheeks.

"That's so you can clean off easier," Cash said. After he finished, he shifted over, lying on his side while Jaye unfolded himself and went to use the sink.

"Thanks, Cash," Jaye said with a small smile. "I appreciate what you're doing for me. I'll make it worth it for you. Promise."

"I know you will, Johnny," Cash replied with a contented sigh.

Chapter 12
Corpse or Whore

After so long without sex, craving it, begging for it, and not getting it because Kris was kind of a prude, it was a rough adjustment period for Jaye. Cash wasn't lying or exaggerating when he'd said he wanted sex every night, then a blowjob each morning.

A few days passed and a routine slowly took form. Servicing Cash's big dick was Jaye's job now, and each day revolved around it, no exceptions. Sometimes it sent Jaye into a mini-panic, to think this was going to be his life now, but when the ghosts of his attackers came out at night or when his guard was down, he was reminded how it could be a lot worse. He could just be a smear of gore on the asphalt behind his old apartment building, or tossed in the dumpster there. But he was alive, and even if he didn't have anyone else to live for, he wanted to find a way to come through his sentence in mostly one piece so it could all be worth something someday.

It was morning. Any minute now all the cells in his unit would open automatically by a switch at the guard station. They'd be sounding the call for showers, getting everyone up and out. Cash was sitting on the side of Jaye's cot, leaning back with his hands braced on the bed top and his pants pulled down to mid-thigh. Kneeling between Cash's feet, Jaye had most of Cash's dick buried in his mouth and throat, his chin covered in saliva. His hand twisted on the shaft each time he pulled back. Cash was watching attentively, enjoying the show with a vaguely condescending smirk on his face. Once in a while, Cash would brush the hair out of Jaye's face, pulling him gently down on the in-stroke, sliding easily into Jaye's throat.

Jaye tried, somehow, to ignore where he was or what was going on around him. He tried not to think or feel anything other than sincere gratitude for Cash's protection. Down the hall, several other cells were opened up first. The occupants wandered down the hall with their toothbrushes, towels and toiletries.

Of course they looked, or he figured they did. He couldn't say because he refused to see for himself. He just kept his focus on Cash. Sucking, grunting softly when the head hit the back of his throat the wrong way, Jaye knew he looked like a shameless whore.

There was a bang on the outside of their cell door. There was a buzz and the door swung open.

"Larson. Jones. Knock that shit off and get to the showers."

Jaye didn't stop, even though the guard had ordered it. It wasn't Dorrance, but Montega, who Jaye noticed would sometimes ignore consensual sexual activity, even though all sexual activity between prisoners, or prisoners and guards, was against the rules. Montega wouldn't put up with it, though, if there was a chance he might get in trouble for giving them a pass. Other guards, unfriendly ones, were likely nearby.

But Montega didn't call the shots with Jaye. Cash did.

In fact, instead of knocking it off, Jaye picked up the pace to try to get Cash to come, worried about what it would mean for him if he didn't fulfill his morning obligations. Cash's hand rested on top of Jaye's head, guiding it steadily up and down on his dick.

"Let's go!" the guard said angrily. "Last warning, Jones. Get your dick out of that kid's mouth. Now."

Cash laughed and pushed Jaye off of him. He pulled up his pants and tucked himself away.

"Yes, sir," Cash said with a tone of feigned humility. Jaye struggled to get off of his aching knees. The cement floor had been grinding into them for a good ten minutes. "Come on, Johnny. We'll finish this later."

He ushered Jaye forward with a hand on his back.

Jaye quickly grabbed his shit and left the cell, as ordered.

From behind Jaye, the guard stopped Cash with a hand to his chest. "We gonna have a problem here?" Montega asked.

"No, sir," Cash smiled. "No problem at all."

The guard's voice got harder to hear as Jaye kept shuffling forward, trying to keep going so he wouldn't get in trouble, but trying to eavesdrop, too.

"He's just a fucking *boy*, Jones. A teenager, for Christ's sake," Montega was saying.

"You don't think I know that?" Cash replied. "Don't worry. I'm watching out for him."

"Doin' a really great job," Montega grumbled.

The showers were crowded when Jaye got there. All he saw was skin and asses. The sound of water beating on ceramic, echoing voices, and the splashing of water filled the air. Dread was a cold finger tracing his spine as he got undressed and stepped into the communal showers, crossing the damp, slimy tile floor.

It was a mixed group. He got a few looks he didn't like, heard a few murmured comments, but then Cash was there, too, and those stopped. The effect Cash had was sort of fascinating.

Jaye glanced back at the bathroom doorway.

Oh shit.

The guard on duty, lingering there, was Dorrance, who'd watched the bathroom while Cash took Jaye's ass for a ride. Jaye just kept moving, though he knew what was coming. He went to use the unoccupied shower Cash pointed him toward, where there were two open side by side. The other guys from Cash's crew were all around them, including Ro, Jaye noted. There were other inmates, also, but mostly it was Cash's guys in that area of the room.

Could be worse. Could be a lot worse.

It was like they knew. Maybe they did. Maybe Cash had said something, promised something, when Jaye wasn't around to hear it.

It happened so gradually, almost like Jaye was imagining it. The other guys crowded around more closely, blocking Jaye from the view of the left side of the showers. Ro's placement in the semi-circle gave him a front row seat. Then Cash moved up behind Jaye.

"Spread your ass, bitch. Show 'em what you got for me," Cash said in a growl from right behind Jaye.

God, he didn't want to. There was no part of him that wanted to follow that order. Not with so many naked, dangerous men watching, becoming aroused, and becoming even more dangerous....

Corpse or whore. Corpse or whore. Take your pick.

He bent over, reached back and spread his cheeks like Cash had asked. The others gathered closer.

"Fuck yeah. Fuck him, Cash," he heard chanted softly around him.

There was pressure as a couple fingers twisted up his hole, and he grunted.

Too many people surrounded him, too many bodies, far too many to fight. Nothing but a spectacle, a joke, a soulless orifice to violate; he started to struggle to breathe. The water was hitting the right side of his face and body, running down the curve of his back and on down the backs of his legs, adding some lubrication as Cash worked him open, fast and rough.

After several pumps, the fingers slid slowly out again until only the tips were inside Jaye. There they stayed, barely inside his rim, spread into a V. It tripped a trigger inside him, the same one Burt had found. Just like that, he was fighting back, trying to get away. Instantly, Cash's hand was wrapped in Jaye's hair, pulling hard on it, enough to force Jaye's head sharply backward. Jaye let go of his ass and braced his hands against the shower wall instead. The pain in his scalp scared him, forming visions of bloody clumps of brown curls yanking violently from the back of his head.

"Shh, easy girl," Cash taunted. Leaning in, he asked calmly, "Do I need to ask my friends to hold you down?"

"No," Jaye grunted, pushing down, hard, on the panic.

"Oh, come on, boss, let us spread that bitch for ya," someone asked with a chuckle.

"I'm fine." Jaye promised.

The pulling on his hair eased slightly, but didn't go away completely. Jaye was careful not to move his head, to make it look like Cash was still yanking as hard as he had been. Then the fingertips popped through his rim to pry it apart again, and he knew they were all looking, maybe with their cocks in hand, ready to step up and have at it, one after another after another.

Jaye's face was on fire, his lungs stone, refusing to expand and accept air. He grunted, softly, with fear and shame. It was mostly real, though he did turn the volume up a little, not trying to hide any of the reaction, since it was the only thing that could convince Cash to be nice to him later, in private.

Laughing, Cash observed, "You really don't like that, do ya? I'm just showing my boys what I bought, right? Letting them appreciate it. This? This is mine. I bought this tight little hole... right here. See that, boys? That's *nice*, isn't it?"

He didn't want to think about who was witnessing this. How Dorrance was standing guard, supervising Jaye's public torture. How Wolf, the burly boy lover, was there, and Ro, the fiftyish biker and Cash's newly promoted third in command, was also there, along with lieutenant Hax, middle-aged hippie, Gravy, and hard-assed Chuckles, and young Jinx, and so many others who surrounded Cash day in and day out. These were men Jaye would be faced with every day, for the rest of his time in FCI Sheridan. There was no escaping their judgment, knowing they would, each of them, always see him like this — a pathetic, weakling faggot, begging to get reamed out by a mean thug bastard.

The noise turned up in Jaye's head, and he growled, trying to mentally go someplace else. There was no out for him, no escape. This was all he got to have in reality, so he chose fantasy instead. He told himself he was alone, being carried away on the water droplets trickling down the drains in the floor, slipping down the pipes faster and faster, getting farther away by the second as Cash's larger, overheated, hairy body pressed at Jaye's back.

Cash's dick was forcing its way into Jaye, holding him by the hip and the hair. Jaye was still fighting a little, and it wasn't at all fake. The hand yanking at his hair kept him mostly still. Cash finished jamming his dick through the small, barely prepped opening, and Jaye swallowed some of his yelp of pain, hiding his face as his tears started to flow, mixing with the shower spray.

Then it was just grunting, rutting, and murmurs of approval to which he refused to listen from all around him. Cash squeezed a handful of Jaye's ass cheek, grinding into him, putting on an enthusiastic show of how completely he'd tamed his kept boy. No one else touched Jaye, but he couldn't even find comfort in that.

Finally, Cash pulled out. Hot fluid, warmer than the water, sprayed over Jaye's ass, dripped through his crack. Cash left it there and the water was slow to rinse it off.

Jaye was still crying, in a small, quiet way. He was thinking of his mom, of all things, and the way she had looked laying there, on her couch, half-naked and used up. In a deep, private, permanent way, his heart broke a little, then, because there was no difference between them, after all. He wasn't her beautiful little bluebird, and he wasn't free. He was nothing, and no one.

Someone murmured under their breath, "Faggot whore." The sound traveled farther than it might have otherwise in the echo-chamber bathroom.

"Hey! You don't fucking call him that," Cash snapped. "You don't fucking call him *anything*."

Staying turned away from the crowd, Jaye rubbed at his face, washing it off. He sniffled a little to clear his nose and kept his back to the others until he was able to pull himself together. He used the shower spray to try to quickly clean up, feeling watched.

"Johnny. C'mere," Cash beckoned.

He didn't want to go, but he wasn't exactly in a position to argue. Jaye took a deep breath, wiped a hand over his face one last time, and turned. Cash was a few steps away, opposite a guy who'd kind of been at the fringes of things at lunch or when the guys were all together. Jaye didn't even know his name, but the twenty-something guy had brown hair, pasty skin, a big nose and freckles.

"It's your lucky day, kid," Cash told Jaye without breaking eye contact with the guy Jaye didn't know. "You get a free shot at Rat as payback for him running his fucking mouth."

Jaye immediately glanced toward Dorrance, but Dorrance didn't seem to be paying them any attention.

Maybe Jaye would get in trouble if he took the shot.

Honestly, he didn't really care. Plenty of people had called him names in his life, especially with the sort of face, hair, sexual orientation, and poverty-stricken life he'd had. But that was the first time he'd been called a name in prison while getting fucked in front of a room full of people.

And it pissed him off.

Feigning like he was shy, or unsure, Jaye kept his head bowed. He dragged his right thumb over his chin, then swung hard, with all of his rage, before Rat could anticipate the blow.

It connected solidly with Rat's big nose. Jaye felt the snap a half second before Rat yelled in pain.

Rat started to reach up to block his probably broken nose, but Jaye's left was already coming around and caught him in the jaw. The bone slid sideways almost comically, the blood streaming down over Rat's lips and chin from his nostrils. Rat forgot for a moment to block the punches, he was so stunned.

Jaye drove his right fist up through the middle and caught Rat in his meaty gut, driving the air from his lungs.

Someone pulled Jaye back. It was Jinx, one of the younger members of the Disciples, maybe a year or two older than Jaye, and who Cash referred to as Puppy due to his newbie status in the gang. Jinx was cracking up, but not as much as Cash, who was practically doubled over with amusement.

The laughter caught on, spreading fast, until Jaye and Rat were the only ones not joining in. Instead, they just stared each other down.

"Call me a faggot whore one more time," Jaye quietly, politely, asked Rat.

"I really think he wants you to," Jinx snickered.

"I do," Jaye admitted. "I'll bite that fucking bloody nose you've got right off. Know why? 'Cause I don't fuckin' *care*." Jaye spread his arms wide in invitation. The laughter was dying off.

Still collecting himself and grinning, Cash stepped closer to Jaye and said with a nod in his direction. "You know he killed someone? That wasn't even what got him landed in here. And he's a fuckin' *teenager*. So, what do you say, Rat?"

"S-sorry, Johnny," Rat muttered thickly, trying to catch the blood which was now running in watery streaks down the front of his pale, naked body to tint the water swirling down the nearby drain.

"He's got bigger balls than you," Cash told Rat with an arched brow. "Trust me, I checked."

Jinx lost it, cracking up and clapping Jaye on the back. Then he touched fists with Cash. From the doorway, Dorrance finally decided to speak up.

"All right, ladies. Break it up. Kauffman, you need to visit Health Services?"

Rat nodded and went to get a towel.

With Cash's arm looped around his shoulders, Jaye left the showers, moving a little awkwardly because of his limp and sore ass. As he did, he noticed how the others weren't ignoring him or looking at him only as something to fuck. Instead, now there was a small sharp glint of approval when he'd catch someone's eye. That's when Jaye knew he had to keep hitting back if he wanted to rise up.

Chapter 13
Crying Johnny

"What if this fucks up my face? Like an infection?"

Cash shrugged, giving him a brief, unfazed glance before he resumed preparing the ink and modified tattoo machine, built from spare contraband parts acquired through trade from other inmates. The needles and ink came through the same sources Cash used to get the drugs and cigarettes inside for the Disciples. Jaye didn't know what those were yet, or how Cash got things inside, but he knew he did. Cash controlled the flow of all goods and services for the Disciples.

Cash had some liner needles, as well as flats for shading, but only had blue or black ink. His set-up was not nearly as professional or sanitary as the tattoo shop where Jaye had his blue jay and tribal piece done. At the same time, it was a lot better than he'd expected.

The tattoo machine, needles, and inks were usually stashed inside the plate of the electrical outlet box in the cell's corner, on the same wall as the bunks. The box was out of the way, and you had to crouch down behind the bunks to see it, so it didn't usually get scrutinized during random searches, and the drug sniffing dogs Jaye had seen them use to find contraband didn't pick up on it either.

"On your list of priorities, how high is staying pretty?" Cash countered.

Jaye grunted in reply. Cash had a point. If the teardrop tattoo turned into a scar, maybe that wasn't a bad thing either. It was a given Jaye could go to sick call and request to be seen by the medical staff if infection set in. Plus, it wasn't like he could hide an infection if one set in right next to his eye. Everyone would see it.

"I won't lose my value if my face gets fucked up?"

Cash laughed softly, eyes downcast as he focused on his work. He tested the machine and seemed satisfied after it began to buzz softly for a moment. The machine was Frankensteined together with tape and rubber bands, which didn't exactly set Jaye's mind at ease either.

"Sit your ass down." Cash pointed to the spot next to him on the top bunk, where the angle would hide them from view a little more than on Jaye's lower bunk.

Once Jaye was settled, faced forward with his legs hanging off the side of the bed and leaned back against the wall, Cash dipped the needles in the blue ink and said, "Johnny, if you meet a guy in here who's only interested in the smoothness and quality of your skin, you run the fuck the other way, you got me? It ain't exactly your face they're interested in. You know that."

Jaye surrendered a little more. He'd always wished he had less of his mother's prettiness and more of a manlier appearance. Now he had a chance to choose for himself what he would look like for the rest of his life. He wanted—no, *needed*—to own what he'd done to Burt McCurdy. It would be the first step of many in his quest to silence his traumatized conscience. There was no part of him that wanted to deny what he'd done. Hiding it would have been harder to live with than wearing it right on his face, for everyone to see. Let them judge him for the truth, instead of what they thought they knew about him.

Jaye had tied his hair back in a bun for once, to keep it out of the way. He tried to stay still as Cash raised the ink-dipped needles to the tender skin below the outer corner of Jaye's left eye.

"Don't fuckin' move." Cash fired up the tattoo machine and touched the buzzing end to Jaye's skin.

The grouping of liner needles bit through. It stung. Eyes shut, controlling the instinct to flinch or frown, Jaye tried to keep his face relaxed. He repeated to himself, like a mantra, 'Man up.' That was the only way he'd get through this without freaking out.

The needles shifted only slightly, drawing their careful line. The moment was intense, worse than when he'd gotten his other two tattoos, which were both fairly massive, and even with how sensitive the area above his cock had been. The reasons why had nothing to do with pain, but more from how cobbled together the tattoo machine was. It was also because of how close to Jaye's eye the needles were.

"You wanna be something more than a pansy little piece of ass, right?"

"Right."

"You want some fuckin' respect, from everyone, from the moment they lay eyes on you, without having to say one goddamned thing?"

"Yeah. I do."

Shifting, constant scratches at his skin left a permanent trail behind. He couldn't see it, but he could feel it burning, throbbing.

Too late to stop now.

Faint reactions stirred. Ripples from a former reality — concerns about how Jaye's customers at the store would look at him, curiosity about whether Kris would like the teardrop, and guesses about the nature of the expression that would cross Cora's beautiful face, seeing what kind of monster her baby had turned into. All of it was dead and cold. Each mental picture of things he'd never have to deal with ever again — his job, his boyfriend, his family — he tore them up and burned them down to ashes.

The harder he pushed them all away, the safer he knew he'd be.

Now, he belonged to Cash. More than that, he belonged to himself. Nobody else mattered. They'd all left him to rot or die.

Little did they know he wasn't going down that easy.

The more the needles scratched open his skin, leaving ink behind, the more the pain sunk in deeper. But it was a small piece. It was over quickly.

Before they'd started, Cash had shown Jaye some of his work, and the tattoos he'd given himself, not to mention some of the other guys in his crew. It turned out Cash had a little artistic talent. Jaye had always loved to sketch. Drawing had been an escape and stress relief throughout his childhood, so whenever he discovered someone he knew had a similar talent, he was impressed.

Cash had one of the most crucial abilities for any tattoo artist to have. He could draw a straight line. More than that, he could cleanly capture an image without having to stencil it onto the skin first. Everything Cash did was freehand, and he was good enough at it that his subjects trusted him completely.

Cash had even done the tears on his own face, which had impressed Jaye more than the clock with no hands on his left forearm, symbolic of the long prison sentence he'd been given, and the meaninglessness of the passage of time behind bars. The open tears were small, requiring a very steady hand and attention to detail.

With his work complete, Cash sat back and admired Jaye's tear with a tight nod. Then he started to pack up his stuff so he could hide it in the electrical outlet box again.

"Take a look in the mirror. Leave it alone for an hour or two, then wash it off with soap and water. Just keep it clean."

Jaye climbed down from the bunk, slipping his foot onto the metal bar step in the frame. He was a little afraid to look at himself in the small mirror above their sink. Whatever he'd see when he did would be something he was stuck with for the rest of his life, however long that would be.

He didn't hesitate, though. Heart beating harder, he stepped up to meet his reflection.

As soon as he saw it, he started to smile.

For months, Jaye had been weighed down by his circumstances, and it showed in his expression, his posture, and his body language. The tear slipping from the corner of his left eye was a symbol of his misery. Somehow, seeing it there, permanently, lifted some of the responsibility from his shoulders. It spoke for him — that he'd been through hell and he'd fought his way out, all on his own.

Sure, maybe it was ugly, but his life was ugly too. There was no reason to strive for perfection or normalcy anymore. He was in the wild. The tattoo was his war paint.

He fucking loved it.

After admiring the new ink, he turned and said to Cash, "Thanks. It's awesome."

In response, Cash clutched his chest and acted choked up, saying, "My little boy's all grown up."

Jaye couldn't help but laugh. Biting his lip to hide the smile he felt all the way down to his toes, he said, "Shut the fuck up."

Cash climbed down from his bunk, quickly hiding the tattoo gear.

When he straightened up again, he asked, "Can I tattoo my name on your ass next?" Cash grinned crookedly, chuckling a little, too, to let Jaye know he wasn't serious.

The funny thing was, Jaye could totally imagine it. Shaking his head and holding up his hands, he said, "Nope. No fucking way. My ass is worth more than my face. Plus, the last thing I need is the word 'Cash' written on my butt when I've already got people calling me a whore."

"Oh, come on," Cash teased. Drawing a shape in the air with his hands, he said, "Then how about a portrait of the original J.C.?"

Jaye burst out laughing. He couldn't help it. "You're not drawing Johnny Cash on my ass, you crazy fucker!" Jaye laughed again, kicking at Cash's leg.

Cash caught Jaye's waist and came at him. Pressing him back against the wall behind Jaye, Cash gave him a hard, deep kiss.

Jaye was too shocked to react at first. They'd never kissed before.

Once the fight response faded away, he began to kiss Cash back, brushing his mouth lightly with his lips and moaning softly. Cash angled his head to go deeper, palming Jaye's ass and slipping Jaye his tongue. Shivers shot down Jaye's spine and through his legs. The affectionate intimacy and passion he was feeling from Cash started to make Jaye hard.

Bang, bang.

"Knock it off!" a guard yelled at them. After a quick glance, Jaye saw it was Coleman, a short, stocky, homophobic guy, and a big stickler for the rules.

Cash backed off, still watching Jaye's mouth. It was clear from the look on his face that they weren't done. Not by a mile. And that was fine with Jaye.

A couple of weeks passed. Time wasn't moving as slowly as it had been, but it wasn't exactly speeding by, either. Most of Jaye's fear dissipated, replaced by a numb sort of acceptance. He still constantly watched his back whenever he wasn't confined to his cell, which was pretty exhausting. Rationally, he knew Cash would watch out for him, but since he didn't have a whole lot of hard proof of the fact to help reassure him, Jaye didn't completely rely on the connection.

Still, his alone time with Cash was becoming something Jaye

looked forward to instead of dreading. The sex itself stopped hurting as his body adjusted, and Cash became more attentive than Jaye had ever expected the guy to be. For instance, Cash always made sure Jaye got off first. He also went out of his way to make Jaye as comfortable as possible.

In a way, though, liking the sex made it a little harder for Jaye to wrap his mind around it. He felt especially guilty about liking sex that was always public to some extent. It wouldn't be a private act again until Jaye had served his time.

Jaye was still responding to it all like he was still his former self, pre-incarceration. He'd detached from his old identity, but hadn't found a new one to claim. Floating along at Cash's side, human property and frequently used, it was surreal, to say the least. Some mornings, Jaye still woke up half expecting the whole thing to have been a weird dream he'd emerge from, back in his old apartment with a wicked hangover.

It was mid-morning. Cash hadn't been around for the past hour or so. That wasn't completely unusual. Cash worked on the janitorial crew, whereas Jaye had signed onto Mechanical Services, studying to work with the Electrical crew. Because they were assigned to different departments, they had different shifts, at different hours and locations.

Ever since that day in the showers when Jaye had broken Rat's nose, Rat hadn't given Jaye any more problems. He hadn't really been coming anywhere near him either. Jaye was sitting at a small table with Kett and Gravy in the recreation room, watching—but not really watching—the small television bolted to the wall. It was showing some public access version of the Judge Judy show, only it wasn't Judge Judy, it was some other woman with bad makeup and a thick New Jersey accent.

Every time someone walked past, Jaye felt like they were looking at his new tear. Sometimes that was just paranoia, but mostly it wasn't. The extra attention was fine with him, though. Let them look. That was the whole point anyway—to send a message.

The ghosts of his attackers hadn't been bothering him as much lately, either. It had been pretty quiet.

Maybe too quiet.

"Larson!" Dorrance called from the main exit, by the hallway which led to the cafeteria, the administrative offices, visitation rooms, inmate phones, and the administrative segregation corridors.

"Yo, man, that's *Johnny*," Gravy argued from Jaye's left. "Ain't no *Larson*."

The rise to his defense made Jaye smile. He nudged Gravy's shoulder as he stood, holding his bad side out of habit more than need. Gravy held out his closed fist and Jaye touched it with his own.

Jaye walked over to where Dorrance was waiting, avoiding eye contact and looking bored. A pair of cuffs were fastened on, loosely enough for Jaye to be comfortable, but not able to slip them either. The center connecting chain led down to another pair of cuffs Dorrance fastened around Jaye's ankles.

Without a word of explanation, Dorrance let Jaye shuffle out through the doorway, then secured the door behind them. The lock engaged loudly.

Did I do something?

Maybe they heard from Mom.

Or maybe they found her.

He wanted to ask, but didn't at the same time.

I'll find out either way. Better to just wait and see.

"Come on." Dorrance took hold of Jaye's upper arm and led him along.

They went past the offices and other likely destinations along the corridor, moving toward the doorway leading to administrative segregation, otherwise known as solitary or the hole, and Jaye started to become more nervous. Tattoos were illegal. It was right there in the handbook.

Are they going to put me in solitary for my tear? Do they know Cash was responsible? Is Cash already there?

"Everything okay?" Jaye asked. Dorrance had a deal going with Cash. Maybe the reason for their trip had something to do with that. The idea should have been more comforting than it was.

Dorrance didn't say anything or even look over, so Jaye shut up, too. The last thing he wanted was to get in even more trouble.

Jaye had never been to ad-seg before, but he'd heard about it plenty. Searching his thoughts, he kept coming up empty when looking for some reason for why he'd be taken there, other than the tattoo. But they wouldn't throw him in solitary for that, would they? He hadn't done anything else wrong. If they knew about the sex with Cash, they wouldn't punish him for it, would they?

Confused and uneasy, Jaye just kept moving. The last thing he wanted was to make things worse by mouthing off or putting up a fight.

Soon, they were in what had to be the ad-seg corridor. The doors were blue and windowless, with only a small slot that could be opened and closed. There were occupants in some. He could hear dull noises like shouting, banging, and singing. The singing was especially creepy.

"Why'd you bring me here? What's going on?" The questions popped out, bursting from his rising panic like foam.

Dorrance pulled a key from the ring clipped to his side and went to unlock one of the cells. The key was in the lock when Dorrance said with a sly grin and a sleazy sort of roaming gaze, "Payback time, princess."

Chapter 14
Gang Bang Movie Star

Just like in the alley behind his old apartment during the attack that got him locked up in the first place, Jaye was forced to make some decisions pretty damned quickly once he was pushed into the cell.

First, he scanned the small room, outfitted much differently than a typical administrative segregation cell. There was a metal table in the middle of the room instead of a cot against the wall. There were also two men in street clothes holding video cameras, standing in the corners on opposite ends of the same wall.

Cash was there. Jaye's focus wanted to linger on him, but instead it snapped around to Hax, Lieutenant of the Disciples, on Cash's left, with his shaved head, bright blue eyes and the tattoos peeking out the edges of his khaki-colored regulation clothing at his neck and wrists. On Cash's right was Jinx, who was only a few years older than Jaye, but strong and eager to follow orders given by full members of the crew in order to earn his place. A guard Jaye didn't know was behind them. The guard looked to be in his late twenties, with caramel-colored skin, a strong jaw, dark, unreadable eyes and a mean look.

There were way too many people.

Behind Jaye, Dorrance closed and secured the cell's door, with both of them now locked inside with everyone else.

It was only the presence of Cash and the cameras, which seemed to be on and recording everything, that helped to convince Jaye he wasn't in mortal danger.

Finally, Jaye bypassed the base survival stage of his reaction and began to engage in more complex thought.

This was payback. This was what Cash had warned him about.

They'd get lube and they'd be left alone when Dorrance was on shift. In exchange, Jaye would get fucked on camera.

They were about to film a porno. A gang bang.

Everyone was silent and still for a long moment, possibly reacting to the tense, mad, scratch-their-eyes-out look that was probably on his face.

The need to do everything in his power to fight to the death to get the hell out of there was so intense, it froze him at first.

But all that was waiting for him if he got out of that cell was more threats, and a bigger likelihood of a grisly death.

He was fucked either way.

It's not a snuff film. Just porn.

You can do this.

Fuck or die.

It'll be hell, but you'll live. You'll earn your protection.

It didn't matter that he wanted to leave. He was there. There was no escape.

He had to role-play this bitch.

The best part was that he knew, as long as he was role-playing, he could mask his real fear behind the pretend version. Let them think he was just going along with it, doing his part. No one — not even Cash — needed to know about the rest, and how petrified he really was.

"What the fuck is this?" Jaye barked at Dorrance with an angry glare. "I thought the whole point of seg was to *segregate* you from everyone else. I shouldn't even be here, anyway. I didn't do anything!"

Jaye shared a look with Cash, letting it linger. Cash nodded to him very subtly.

"You know you owe us."

"The fuck I do!"

Dorrance shoved Jaye from behind, knocking him off of his feet and flying forward. Cash and Hax caught him, then pushed him roughly over the side of the table. The chain connecting Jaye's wrists to his ankles pulled around the table's metal edge, forcing him to bend over sharply, his arms yanked downward.

"Get your fuckin' hands off me!" Jaye yelled, fighting back enough to put on a good show for the cameras. "Don't touch me!"

His pants were pulled down to his ankles. Someone's fingers

twisted up his ass. Two of them, from what Jaye could tell. He growled with ache and anger, louder than he ever would have naturally. In his peripheral vision, he saw one of the camera guys move in for a closer shot. It made Jaye a little nauseous to think about that, and what the camera's eye saw, so he tried to tune it out.

"I don't think you're in charge right now," Cash said lightly, in his gruff growl of a voice. The fingers pulled out, then hooked in him from either side, pulling his hole open. He grunted thickly, and that was mostly real, the ghosts trying to creep up and twist in the gray matter of his brain until the panic was strangling him senseless.

"Been watching you," Dorrance said. "We see how much you love cock, so we're gonna give you some. Aren't we?"

Bowing his head, Jaye closed his eyes. He forced himself to take a deeper breath to try to calm down. He didn't want to know where the cameras were, or where the other players in the room were. It was bad that it wasn't just Cash, or Cash and one guard. There were just too many and, with the exception of the other guard, they were all people Jaye *knew*. They were men he would have to look in the eye every single day, no matter what happened in that cell before they finished with him.

What the fuck are they planning to do to me?

"Your ass has some stretch to it, princess," Dorrance said with an amused lilt to his voice. "You been someone's whore lately?"

The fingers were still stretching his hole when another finger slid right through, between them. It was wet and cold.

It startled him enough to provoke a cry of pure shock. A hard shudder of revulsion ran down his back. It wasn't just Cash touching him, like he was used to. It could have been anyone.

"Stop!" Jaye yelled, his voice cracking like he was fifteen instead of nineteen. "Please! Please don't!"

"Shut that bitch up. Be creative."

The other guard and Jinx came over. More hands held him down. Bodies rearranged themselves around Jaye. Hax walked around the table, pulling his pants down in front to free his dick. It already had a rubber on it.

Fear was a push.

Jaye tried to straighten up, to scramble backward, but several strong men held him down. No matter how hard he struggled, he didn't budge an inch, though his rough yells grew in volume and strength.

"Get away from me! Get the fuck away!"

Wearing an unreadable expression, almost like he'd glazed over and detached from what he was actually doing, Hax came right up to Jaye; Hax, who had daily, for weeks, smiled at Jaye from across the table in the dining hall, and sometimes gave him a reassuring little pat on the back as he passed by. Like Jaye was a stranger instead of the teenage kid who'd been tagging along next to his boss, he pinched Jaye's nose shut. Then, Hax waited for Jaye to open his mouth while Hax stroked himself hard.

It would have been better if it was guys I didn't know.

But Cash doesn't trust anyone else. You know that. He wouldn't let anyone other than his boys touch you.

Hax warned, "You know you don't want me to feel any of those teeth, right? I don't think you'd like the way I'd keep that pretty mouth open. If you accidentally broke your jaw, there'd be no solid food for a long, long time." Hax laughed. To Jaye it sounded hollow, which somehow didn't help. It only made Jaye want to cry.

Hax was in his late twenties, maybe twenty-nine. There was only a decade between them, but Hax had a look to him that hinted at the damned path he'd followed to end up where he had. He'd had a hard life, which Jaye knew nothing about. All Jaye knew was Hax had done Cash's dirty work for a while now. That glazed expression was a tool in his arsenal to get the job done.

Now the job was Jaye.

The blood wanted to run right out of Jaye body. He started to tremble.

That third finger was still up his ass, twisting around and pushed in to the last knuckle. The unwanted, searching touch was making Jaye frantic. He couldn't stop trying to bear down or silence the terrified, broken, constant cries he was making. He hated it. The instinct was to grab for a weapon—any weapon—and fight his way free just to get the touching to stop. He would have if he could have, even if it meant hurting Cash or his crew.

The finger searched and bent, rubbing deliberately over his prostate gland.

Jaye let out a startled whimper, convulsing, his hips snapping forward. The finger just followed along and kept at it while they chuckled at his reaction.

"That's it," Dorrance purred. "Found that sweet spot, huh? How's that feel, princess? You like that?"

Hax's dick was right in Jaye's face. Jaye had opened up with the whimper, so Hax slid his dick right back over Jaye's tongue, his nose still pinched tightly shut. The cockhead nudged his throat the wrong way and he gagged. Maybe liking the reaction, or trying to bypass it, Hax just pushed in deeper. One of the cameras was right there, inches from Jaye's face. He wouldn't look at it, but he couldn't pretend he didn't know how close it was. That black, glass eye stared, unblinking and hungry, at the mouth rape.

Thrusting in and out, shallowly, Hax moaned, putting on a show of his own. It still sounded false, in a bad way. It hinted that Hax wasn't totally on board with this, but wouldn't protest, or stop. Jaye tried not to care, to just act like a scared kid who'd never sucked cock before. He didn't have to make it good for Hax or the camera. He just had to let it happen.

The unknown guard said, "Ready to fuck that hole? Give this pretty boy a ride from both ends?"

Jaye was being held down by two sets of hands. Someone was playing with his rim while someone else's finger was buried there, milking him. Too many people surrounded him, touching him exactly where he least wanted them to. He had a dick down his throat, fingers moving in and out of his ass, and everyone could see. Everyone wanted in.

Jaye moaned, "No," but the word was only a mumble around the engorged cock stuffing his mouth, using his throat.

"Yeah," Hax sighed, caressing Jaye's jaw as he thrust. "Suck it. Suck my cock, bitch."

Go someplace else. You went to a club to hook up. That's all this is. You got lonely and you're just hooking up. You'll get off and go home to your own bed. You've gotta get some sleep for work tomorrow.

Someone was standing right behind him. The fingers were out of his ass. He felt what had to be a dick pressing to enter him. Strangely, he was comforted by its large size.

Cash.

He remembered he was role-playing.

Just role-playing.

At least he didn't have to say anything. He tried not to tense up so it wouldn't hurt as much.

He gasped loudly when Cash breached him, easing past his outer ring. Then Hax pushed in too far, stuffing Jaye's throat, cutting off his air. The ache in Jaye's ass flared as the panic of not being able to inhale made him buck. More hands held him down, kept him still and impaled at both ends.

The longer Jaye was choked like that, the less he was able to control his natural fight response. The more he fought, the more he tensed and the more it hurt as Cash burrowed deeper.

"He's a fighter, ain't he?"

"That's all right. He's not going anywhere. He'll learn to like it."

Hax didn't pull his dick out of Jaye's throat until Cash was fully seated. When, finally, Jaye inhaled, he filled his lungs in one huge gulp of blessed oxygen. He stopped fighting, and just lay there, enjoying the ability to breathe.

He could see the unknown guard to his left side. The guard bent over Jaye, spreading Jaye's ass with both hands, squeezing the muscle. Dorrance was on the other side of the table and had his fingers in Jaye's hair, combing it back with his fingers, pulling on a handful of strands to force his head back more. That meant it was probably Jinx that Jaye felt holding him down. Each of Cash's thrusts pushed Jaye gently into the edge of the table.

Just role-playing.

Gonna slice open your belly. Pull your insides out. Make you watch.

No.

"Yeah, that's it. Give it to 'im."

Hax started going harder once Jaye gave his dick a suck to urge him on, even if it wasn't in character. Jaye didn't care. He just wanted it to be over.

The cock began to ride his mouth a little faster. The one up his ass gave him a slower ride, and Jaye was thankful for it. The last thing he wanted was to get torn up back there.

The cameras moved around him, getting different angles. One moved in on a tighter shot of his ass. The other had a wider shot of the view by his mouth. There were eerie, faint mechanical whirs as the lens zoomed in and out. The unknown guard stepped back to give them a better shot of the inmates double-teaming Jaye.

"Come on his face," the guard told Hax.

"No," Cash growled. It wasn't in character, and there were no reasons for it other than selfish ones. Jaye was so thankful, he cracked a smile.

Three more pushes and Hax came with a satisfied groan.

He pulled out.

"Go ahead, Torez," Dorrance said. The unknown guard, Torez, took Hax's place.

Jaye tried as hard as he could to shut down and feel nothing, know nothing. Torez wasn't rough with him as Jaye's mouth was fed another cock, but it was the idea of what was happening that Jaye couldn't bear. His mouth was getting dry from the rubbing of the latex.

He didn't want Cash to come. He really didn't.

But Cash did come, and without pulling out.

When he withdrew, he left Jaye feeling strangely empty.

A hand slapped his ass, hard. Two fingers rubbed his rim and he was spanked again, and again. Jaye was grunting, the dick pumping down his throat, stretching out his lips around its circumference.

"Been waiting to get a piece of this, Johnny," Dorrance sighed. "Let's see what all the fuss is about, huh?"

Another slap to his right cheek, this one hard enough to make Jaye sob a little with the pain.

Then there was pressure. He grunted, fought, and it was real. It wasn't role-play at all. With all of his remaining strength, gathering it up and pushing it, hard, into his need to get free, Jaye bucked and wrestled against all of those hands pinning him down. A muffled scream broke free. He reacted like it was a filleting knife instead of a dick pushing through his sphincter. The others renewed their hold. Someone was laughing.

That it was a guard, an enemy, shoving his dick up Jaye's ass, caused the swell of horror and primal terror. It grew so big, all Jaye knew for a while was the nightmare of the pressure of being force-fucked, and the fight.

The dick went through his rim and burrowed deeper. He tried to push it out, grunting thickly. A few tears slipped down his cheeks. His face was hot, the tension and panic making his head throb with an instant headache, his body clenched and tight, doing everything to push back against the many hands and the pair of dicks sticking into him. There were too many men, too many touches in too many places. The multitude of fingers and palms grabbing at him and pressing on him drew out Jaye's demons. They reached into his intestines, pulling out bloody loops to pile on the floor beneath the table. They wriggled in his brain, screwing it up. Their voices gained in strength, too, feeding on his frenzied energy. Jaye screamed again and they only mocked him louder.

Look at him go!

Look at him dance! He fuckin' loves it.

Faggots like you love to feel things sticking way inside here, don'cha? You like that? You like to get poked? You're a fucking monster. You know what we do to monsters? Little faggoty ones like you? We give 'em what they want!

Tugging at his shackled arms, wanting to cover his ears, his wrists slammed up against the edge of the table beneath him. He tried to shake his head, but Torez had it in a tight, two-handed grip.

He yelled around the cock in his mouth, shouting, "Stop! No!" The muffled protests only made Torez use him more roughly, jamming the column of his dick at the insides of Jaye's cheeks, the roof of his mouth, making him retch as it slammed into the back of his throat. The cock fucking his ass gave it hard and fast, pounding into him. Jaye never stopped fighting it. Cash, Hax and Jinx seemed to all be holding him down. Behind him, Dorrance was moaning happily and scratching up the skin of Jaye's ass, thighs and lower back.

"Oh yeah," Dorrance groaned, nailing him too hard. "Mmm, keep it up, sugar. The more you squirm, the more you squeeze and it feels *so good....*"

It went on too long.

Torez finished with Jaye's mouth. He stepped back and left Jaye to collapse onto the tabletop. Trying to catch his breath, Jaye wished his hands were free to dry his face. He couldn't fight anymore. He hid his face against the metal tabletop as the camera panned in to get a shot of his tears. The edges of his vision were blacking out, his head spinning and his muscles failing him. So, he went into his head instead. Boneless and bent-over where they held him, he lay there, lifeless. His body was nudged forward regularly with the thrusts inside him.

He wasn't in Oregon; he was on the coast of Alaska, standing at the water's edge. Kris had slept in, but Jaye woke early to see the sun rise. Strolling by himself along the water's rocky edge, he felt the spray from the waves on his skin. The wind whooshed in his ears. He skipped stones against the sea's surface, disturbing it in ripples of amber gold, watching them shiver and still over and over again.

Somewhere else, Dorrance pulled out and came over Jaye's ass.

They stopped holding him down, but his body stayed where it was, his mind still elsewhere.

Torez left with Jinx, Hax, and the cameramen. The door shut heavily behind them. It was the heavy metallic slam that roused him.

A sob rose in Jaye's throat and it took everything he had to fight it back down.

"Clean him up," Dorrance told Cash.

"You all right, Johnny? You hurt?"

A hand lightly touched his side, just trying to get his attention. Jaye jumped away from the contact, straightening a little and stumbling over his shackled feet. His knees felt too weak to support him. Panting, sweat-drenched, and woozy, he backed into the corner of the room. He slid down to crouch with his back to the walls.

They both moved to approach him.

"STAY THE FUCK AWAY!"

His ravaged voice broke apart, shifting into a wheeze. They stopped. Cash raised his hands.

"You did good, Johnny," Cash said. To Dorrance, he added, "Debt's paid now, right?"

"Right," Dorrance nodded.

Cash moved forward again. Jaye flinched wildly, ready to try his best to fight him off, shackles be damned, but Dorrance stepped up as well. They both yanked him to his feet without any trouble.

"We need to get out of here, kid. We'll clean you up; get you back where you belong. Okay?"

Jaye couldn't breathe, couldn't stop trying to fight them. He kicked at a leg, tried to bite a hand.

"Knock it off! You quit that and I'll take the cuffs off," Dorrance said.

It was no use. It was over anyway. They'd had him and they would again if they wanted. There was nothing he could do to stop it. Giving up in more ways than one, Jaye drooped, hanging his head, letting them take his weight.

The cuffs came off.

He wanted to take a bite out of Cash when he touched Jaye's back, trying to lead him to the sink. He wanted to stomp on Dorrance's balls until they popped.

But he didn't do any of that. He stayed numb and slack as they washed him off and pulled up his pants.

They led him back out of the cell, then the corridor. The further they went, the more Jaye had to rely on Dorrance's brutal grip on his arm to keep him on his feet.

Normalcy returned, unwanted.

The rest of the day passed in a haze. Hearing people who weren't there, feeling fingers on and in him when he was being left alone, Jaye kept fighting an entirely inner battle. Jaye went where he needed to, according to the prison's daily schedule, but he paid no notice to what happened around him. The more hours that passed, the more every-thing inside shut down.

That night, Cash climbed into his bed like he usually did, without saying a thing. Hours of numbness had worn away the anger Jaye'd felt in that damned cell in solitary. Routine took over. He knew they didn't want to make noise and alert any of the unfriendly guards to what was happening. Jaye was able to begin to go through the mo-tions even with all of the rage, grief, shame, and shock twisting him up inside. There was a chasm between his body and his mind. All that filled the gap, were echoes.

Cash settled on top of Jaye, who was lying on his stomach, sliding under the sheet and blanket with him. Without turning to make eye contact, Jaye drew his legs up. He pushed his pants down past his ass. Cash caressed Jaye's back, then slipped two lube-slicked fingers into him. Jaye bowed his head, staying quiet, too worn out to be tense. He didn't wanted to be touched at all, to just be left alone, but knew he didn't have a say.

This was his life now. This was what he had worked so hard to attain.

Safety.

It could be worse. What happened in that cell could be every day instead of just once.

At least Cash is nice to me when we're alone.

There was a line drawn between them now, though. Maybe Cash wouldn't let anyone touch Jaye without permission. But if they did have permission, then obviously Cash didn't give a fuck.

Cash gave Jaye a third finger. Jaye's breath caught as he started to get choked up, feeling sorry for himself in the most pathetic way possible.

Because he couldn't say no. He'd relinquished the right. The next two years, minus a few weeks, were going to be hell.

Cash shifted, lying more fully on Jaye. There was pressure as Jaye was entered, but no pain.

Jaye started to cry. Cash didn't say anything about it, or even act like he had noticed. But he kept caressing Jaye's sides, breathing heavily against the cascade of his long, curly hair at the side of Jaye's neck, and used his body. He was even more gentle than usual, so maybe that was all right.

It was the last time during Jaye's time in Sheridan that he cried about sex he voluntarily participated in. After that night, Jaye began to lock up the part of himself that could be weak like that and started to build on top of it so that no one could ever hurt him like that again.

Chapter 15
Targeted

Jaye didn't witness the fight, or whatever led up to it. Cash had been working, mopping the halls most likely. A rival gang member, Rico, supposedly said something to Cash in passing. It was hard to get a straight story, even from the guys in the Disciples, since no one had been there but Cash, Rico and the guard, Montega.

All Jaye knew was that one day Cash went off to do his shift at work and didn't come back.

The only thing left to explain his absence were rumblings: Rico had said something to Cash. Cash waited until after his shift, and on his way to the cafeteria for lunch, came across Rico again with some of his crew. Cash had been on his own, but it hadn't mattered. He'd punched Rico in the throat, then kneed him in the balls. Rico went down. Cash stomped on Rico's lower left leg hard enough to snap it.

That was that.

Cash was in ad-seg for real, and Jaye was alone.

It was strange and unsettling to have the cell to himself, spending the morning and evening hours undisturbed. At first Jaye had been a little excited about it—some peace and quiet at last. But he hadn't been fully aware of the ways Cash's presence had been reassuring. There had been a reason, after all, why Jaye had made his deal. Now, his protection was a symbolic presence rather than an actual, living, breathing, scary guy.

Of course Jaye suspected the fight had been because of him. Maybe it was arrogant to think Cash's drama revolved around him, but Jaye had reason enough.

The Disciples didn't give Jaye shit anymore, but they didn't exactly treat him like he was really one of them. They tolerated his presence and kept their hands off, since they knew exactly what Cash would do to them when he got back, otherwise.

There were still plenty of looks thrown his way that gave Jaye the creeps, no matter where he went or what he was doing. Visiting the showers was his least favorite part of the day. As soon as he dropped his towel, he'd feel the room get quieter. The stares would intensify, like they were all mentally playing out fantasy rape scenarios in their heads.

Jaye's second least favorite times were when he'd see the bank of inmate phones or have the opportunity to use one. It was his biggest daily reminder that he didn't have anyone to call or connect to; no ties at all left in the wide world to comfort him.

One day, he stood there, staring at the phones, sleeping quietly in front of him. He ran through the list of people in his head once again; Cora, who had vanished, and was most likely gone for good this time; Kris, that asshole, who didn't actually give a shit after all; his friends from work, like Layla, who'd probably written him off as a murderer; his old neighbors, who'd been friendly enough when he'd been a regular sight in the halls or around town, but now knew him only as that Larson boy who'd gotten himself locked up.

There was still his grandfather on his mom's side, the only pathetic excuse for family Jaye had left. Jaye had only met his grandfather once, for his tenth birthday. Devon Mitchell had been visiting, moved maybe by a freak bout of sentimentality. He'd been a lot older than Jaye had expected—a rickety, elderly man who'd once been strong and fearsome, but still lived way out, in a painstakingly handmade cabin, in the middle of Nowhere, Alaska.

Jaye didn't have a phone number for his grandfather, and even if he did, he wasn't sure what good calling would do. It's not like the guy was likely to come all the way down to Oregon to visit his shameful excuse for a grandson in prison. Hell, he might not even take the phone call once they asked him if he would accept the charges.

But still, Jaye stood there, thinking about it. Maybe he could reach out to his court-appointed lawyer, ask him to look up Devon Mitchell, in Zus, Alaska. The idea of hearing a voice on the other end of that phone line, someone other than a lawyer or a cop or a doctor, would have been really nice. It would have been some assurance that he was still somebody, other than criminal trash and a lot of used-to-bes.

The first time it happened, it was late, after dinner but before lights-out. Jaye was lying on his cot, reading a book. Most of the inmates were out in the common area watching television, playing cards or chess or just hanging around in groups, but Jaye just wanted to be left alone. Without Cash to keep everyone in line, and with plenty of non-Disciples around, it had seemed too dangerous to take the risk of being out there when he could be lying low in his cell.

The daylight was fading, the humming fluorescents above his head casting a harsh, ugly shine on everything. There was a steady hum of conversation, shouts, footsteps scuffing on linoleum, and some singing from the level above. There didn't seem to be many people around where Jaye was. It was quiet.

He heard the footsteps—multiple sets of them—coming down the corridor, but that didn't necessarily mean anything. When three guards stopped at the entrance to his cell, looking right at him, Jaye watched them from over the top of his book, his heart rate picking up speed, fast. The middle guard edged into the room. The other two hung back, blocking the doorway completely.

"On your feet!" the center guard, Ecker, shouted. He was incredibly tall and skinny, like a normal-sized guy who'd gotten freakishly stretched out like taffy and never sprung back into shape. His hair was buzzed short. He had almost no chin and his eyes were sunken.

Jaye set his book down carefully, making sure he didn't lose his place. Then, he stood, raising his hands to shoulder height, palm out, just in case.

Ecker stepped forward, holding his baton. A cold sweat threatened to break out over Jaye's body, inner alarms blaring in his head, when Ecker asked, "Where'd you hide it, Johnny?"

"Wh-what? What are talking about?" Jaye sputtered, feeling lost.

"We know you have it. We've got it on good authority, so where'd you hide it?"

Jaye's heart hammered in his chest. Ecker grabbed the bed covers on Jaye's cot and yanked. His book spilled onto the floor, the pages ruffling as the blanket and sheet were torn free before Ecker flipped the mattress, too. Then he did the same to Cash's cot. After those were both a mess, he turned to their carefully arranged things on the desk and the shelf, knocking them to the floor with the baton.

Breathing harder, hands still raised, eyes too wide, Jaye just stood there, helpless.

"I don't have anything," Jaye tried to say. "I swear! I'm just trying to mind my own business, I—"

"Strip!"

Oh god, no.

The other guards were smiling a little, and Jaye was so terrified, his bladder threatened to let go of its contents. Three guards, one of him. That was bad math.

Hands shaking, Jaye pulled off his shirt. He hesitated just for a second before reaching for his pants. The guards in the doorway only smiled more, but not Ecker. Ecker looked pissed off in a bad way.

"I said strip," he growled.

He was so much taller, Jaye had to crane his neck to see Ecker's face. It made him feel even more like a little kid, with no way to protect himself and in way over his head.

Jaye pushed the pants down and stepped out of them. It took all of his strength not to cover himself with his hands. He was trembling, tensed up, and bracing himself for god knew what.

Ecker grabbed him by the arm, spun him around and shoved him, hard, over to the toilet.

"Grab behind your knees," Ecker demanded.

That big long body with stretched out arms and legs, and unnaturally long fingers was right behind Jaye. There was no part of him that wanted to bend over, naked, in front of that man, but he had no choice. They could claim he was fighting them, beat him bloody, then throw him in solitary along with Cash.

Jaye bent over and grabbed behind his knees, as requested. He was groaning softly with fright, trying so hard to calm down and be cool.

"Where'd you put it?" Ecker asked. "There's only two places it could be, I figure, since it's not in your cell. Think I'll check up here first."

A clammy, dry finger poked right up Jaye's ass, pushing hard to go deep all at once, and Jaye gasped loudly. The finger twisted around and he tried to shut his mouth, but his horror was clawing at his brain, the ghosts of Burt and Earl laughing while they spun a filleting knife that glinted in the light. Ecker rooted around inside Jaye, digging, reaching farther than anyone else ever had and Jaye's knees wanted to give out.

Slowly, the finger pulled out, and two pushed in instead, going farther than Jaye thought fingers could and he made an awful, soft, plaintive noise, just begging. Just wanting it to stop.

"No, don't feel it yet... Better keep searching," Ecker said calmly while Jaye came apart, trembling and pleading wordlessly. "Open your mouth wide. Now. Wide as you can. Now stick out your tongue."

Jaye had no idea what was happening, or what Ecker wanted. The fingers were still up Jaye's ass, buried to the last knuckle, feeling like twelve inches of finger. Ecker reached around Jaye's face with his free hand and stuck two of those fingers between Jaye's lips. Without any hesitation, Ecker slid them down Jaye's throat. Jaye tried to cry out, "No!" but Ecker was too fast, his fingers too long.

Jaye's gag reflex was triggered almost right away as those cool, alien digits filled his throat, rubbing the back of it.

Jaye couldn't stop retching. It was a violent heaving from beneath his stomach as everything in him tried to push out through his mouth. He was leaning over the toilet bowl, so when his dinner came rushing up, it all went in there. The fingers pulled out of his throat while he puked, but the ones in his ass just pumped farther and farther. Remembering Burt, Jaye feared Ecker was trying to grab hold of Jaye's intestines and yank them out.

Ecker looked into the bowl and said, "Nope, still can't find it. Let's try again!" The two other guards laughed.

"No!" Jaye begged, weakly, a moment before the fingers went back down his throat, filling it up, making him retch again as they wriggled in there, jabbing down his esophagus. The panic of trying to breathe, of needing to dislodge those fingers, was maddening. He gagged over and over, his eyes streaming tears, his nose running, and saliva dripping from his quivering lips until he was throwing up again. While it was all coming up, Ecker finger-fucked him with long strokes. The combination made Jaye try to scream, but thick, liquidy sounds interrupted his hoarse yelling.

Before Jaye was even done dry-heaving, the fingers were back down his throat and Jaye whined sharply. It was worse than the attack, because he knew there was no way he'd die. It would just go on and on forever, without end.

"How's that, piggy?" Ecker asked quietly, sliding his fingers all the way out of Jaye's ass, then slipped them all the way back in, provoking an awful, weak protest from Jaye. The fingers in his mouth rubbed around over his tongue and teeth, hooking over his jaw to force it widely open. "How's that smell? You like that? How's that smell?"

The fingers pushed just a little too far back over his tongue and Jaye retched loudly again. It was more dry-heaving. His stomach was empty but that didn't mean it couldn't try. All the way down from his toes, his body tried to force it all out as Ecker encouraged the reaction. Jaye's head was spinning. He couldn't stop the reflexive response because the fingers wouldn't stop pushing down his throat. The finger fucking in his ass got harder, rougher, like Ecker was getting off on it.

"How's that, piggy? I know you like that, piggy. Gonna have some fun with you, huh? Gonna be my little piggy for a long, long time, aren't ya? Yeah, that's right. You like that, huh? You catch that stink, piggy?"

The fingers pulled out of Jaye's mouth. Ecker grabbed the back of Jaye's head, forcing it down, low to the bowl. Jaye fought, or tried to, but the vomiting had left him drained and shaky. The smell went up his nose, got in his head. He tried to push Ecker off, to get away, but he was too exhausted, Ecker too strong.

The fingers pulled out of his ass. Ecker shoved Jaye forward, into the wall. The ends of Ecker's fingers hooked in Jaye's nostrils. Ecker yanked upward with them, forcing Jaye to stand on his toes, pulling Jaye up by those two fingers which smelled like the inside of Jaye's ass. They pushed deeper, lodged painfully in his nose, cutting off his air. Jaye gasped roughly, twisting, trying to push the arm away or pull it down, but unable to budge it.

Behind them, the other pair of guards were still laughing. Ecker chuckled.

"Say thank you, piggy," Ecker warned, the threat obvious in his tone.

"Thank you," Jaye sobbed.

The fingers left his nose and he crumpled to the floor. The guards left. Jaye pulled himself quickly into the corner of the room, curling up there in a ball with his hands over his head, shaking violently and crying for a long time.

There was no calling Cash, no way to reach him. It was just Jaye, on his own. The Disciples couldn't do anything for him without Cash's say so, and especially since Ecker was pretty untouchable. Hax, Cash's second-in-command, said as much.

Jaye had approached Hax in the exercise yard, gathering his pride in order to speak, man to man, with someone who'd so recently taken part in filmed, forced sex with Jaye.

There was no sign, from the look on Hax's face, that he had any recollection of what he'd done to Jaye in solitary. He looked Jaye right in the eye and said, "Hey, Johnny. What's up?"

Hax was younger than he seemed, Jaye knew. There was less than ten years between their ages, but Hax had enough seniority in other ways to more than make up for it.

"Ecker tossed my cell," Jaye said, folding his arms and glancing away first, feeling his face flush with shame. "Said I was hiding something. Did a-a cavity search that was a lot closer to rape than an examination, and forced me to puke, over and over again while him and his buddies laughed. And I don't... Don't know what to do."

"Yeah, he's given other guys shit," Hax said with a slight frown, "'specially the young ones or loners, but he's got it out for the Disciples, too. We'll look into it, but our hands might be tied here. Ecker's single, no family, no friends, no leverage. Just try to stay out of his way, all right?"

"Yeah. Right. Thanks," Jaye said.

Jaye started to avoid hanging out in his cell, alone, like he'd been doing, but that was just trading one danger for another. Inmates or guards. He couldn't even try to go alert someone in charge about

Ecker's behavior, since technically Jaye shouldn't even have been assigned to Cash's cell. It was a favor for a favor, and if he got them digging into his file, they could find evidence of favoritism. The last thing Jaye needed was for Dorrance to get in trouble. He was a big piece of what was keeping Jaye breathing. If Dorrance was suddenly unable to watch out for Cash, then Cash couldn't watch out for Jaye.

Jaye spent every day and night on edge, barely eating, never really resting. One week after Ecker had visited Jaye's cell, he returned.

While the torture was happening, time stopped moving. That single incident lasted for years.

There was no way out of it, no way to pretend it away. Knowing what was coming the second time, Jaye fought harder, which only got him a nasty bruise across the center of his back where the baton whacked him, knocking him into the cement wall and giving him more bruises on his forearms.

Then, while Jaye curled up protectively on the floor, Ecker beat him into submission. Blows landed across his back, legs, arms and side. Jaye stopped fighting.

Bleeding, aching, shaking, he climbed to his feet and stripped down.

For a long time, spidery fingers poked around in his ass, letting him know he was no better than a farm animal. A creature in a cage. And the ghosts whispered to him, right by his ear, *How's that feel, piggy? Gonna slice open your belly. Pull your insides out. Make you watch.*

Then, from the sweaty, imposing body pressed up against his back, Jaye heard, "You like that, piggy? Gonna squeal? Gonna cry? No, I think you like that. If you like it, say thank you."

The voices blended, equally as loud, equally real.

"Thank you," he said hoarsely, his voice in tatters from screaming and protesting.

When two fingers pushed down his throat, he tried to call out for his mother. It was something he knew he would never admit to, no matter what, but he couldn't convince himself it didn't happen, brought so low as to fall back on instincts he hadn't needed since he was a small child fearing the boogeyman hiding under his bed. The cry was lost in his whimpering and retching, for which he was grateful, after.

When the contents of his stomach had been purged and light-headedness threatened to make him collapse into the metal bowl of his own mess, he grasped desperately at the wall, at the sink, anything to keep him upright. His fingers clutched to the pebbled surface of the painted cinderblock wall, to the cold metal edge of the sink. They were strong, unyielding, unlike him. He was moved gently by each push made into him. His mental tethers were slightly stronger than his physical ones, but even those were gossamer thin.

Though the ghosts pried at the ends, his will managed to hold firm until Ecker left again, once forever had passed.

Then, Jaye lay on the floor, naked, sweat-soaked, glassy-eyed, twitching and screaming inwardly at himself to get up, to pull it together. And the ghosts whispered, *piggy, piggy, piggy... time to play. Say thank you.*

Chapter 16
Echoes

That evening at dinner, he felt people staring. He sat on the bench in the dining hall, fork in hand, afraid to eat though his stomach was painfully empty. Gravy asked, "Hey, you okay, Johnny? You don't look too good."

"Fuckin' Ecker, man. Leave the kid alone," Hax replied.

"Cash'll take care of him," Ro told Jaye, trying to sound reassuring or confident.

"Cash is gone," Jaye murmured, not touching his tray of tasteless, gray meat and boiled potatoes.

"What's Ecker's deal, anyway?" young Jinx asked.

Hax brushed his nose, looked around to make sure none of the guards were too close, and said quietly, "Knows about Cash's stash, but doesn't have proof or shit. And he knows Cash ain't talking."

"But Johnny doesn't—"

"I know," Hax cut in, then gave Jaye a sympathetic glance. The warmth behind it never touched Jaye, since he knew there was no hope of salvation. Hax couldn't help. No one could.

Smuggling. That's what it was all about. The Disciples had a source that brought in cigarettes and some drugs, like Ecstasy. That was as much as Jaye knew. He didn't know where Cash kept his stash, but it wasn't in their cell. In the plentiful time Jaye'd had to think it over, he guessed that maybe there were loose tiles or bricks hidden here and there around the building, behind which Cash hid things. Since he was always out there, moving around, cleaning up, it would make sense. That's where Jaye would have kept shit, anyway, and there were too many possible places for the guards to check. They'd never find it without a tip.

But Cash didn't tell Jaye anything. Everyone knew it. Jaye wasn't in the loop. He was a fuck-toy. He was property, just as much as that stash was. Jaye couldn't talk even if he wanted to, and that's just how Cash liked it.

Sure, when Cash got out of solitary, he'd be pissed, and he'd go for payback... or try to. Because Ecker fucking with Jaye was Ecker fucking with Cash.

In the meantime....

"Cash'll be out soon," Ro told Jaye. Ro knew the most about the ins and outs of Sheridan, since he'd been in and out of there himself over a span of twenty years.

"Sure. Soon," Jaye replied.

Three days later, Jinx, Hax and several other members of the Disciples were in the showers with Jaye. Montega was on the door, but when they had almost finished up and began to head out, Ecker took over.

"Larson," Ecker said, stepping in front of Jaye to block his exit. Most of the other guys had already passed by. "Hold up."

Jaye stared at nothing, closing off as many senses and thought processes as he could. It was better to not think about it, to not react. He would just do as he was told. And he suspected the more he fought, the louder the ghosts would get.

"He's with us," Hax argued severely, his tone brusque and forceful.

"No, I don't think so," Ecker grinned. "Move it along or I'll have to write you up."

"Cash is gonna fuck you up, you pervert," Hax hissed.

"What'd you say to me? Come 'ere and say that again," Ecker challenged.

Hax walked away. Jaye appreciated the attempt, but it wasn't anyone's fight but his own. In fact, he was relieved to see Hax go. Even if it meant more pain for himself, Jaye didn't want to see anyone else suffering for him. The Disciples were already missing Cash. They couldn't lose Hax too.

Once they were alone, Ecker yanked Jaye's towel off, then pushed him backward. "Go! Go on! Into the stall. I know you've got it, Johnny. We're gonna keep doing this until you talk. I think I'm gonna find it this time, though. Gonna make sure I do."

Ecker kept pushing Jaye when he didn't move fast enough, and even though he wasn't resisting, sent him careening into the metal walls of the toilet stalls. He ricocheted with a bang and tried to brace himself. There was no fight though. He was too tired to manage it, too resigned.

His bare feet slipped on the wet tile and he fell to the ground, barely catching himself on his hands, lying on his stomach.

"Show me your hands." Ecker stood over him, reaching down with his long, skinny arm, extending his baton.

Before Jaye could try to get up, the baton poked at him. The end was grinding into his spine at his lower back. Jaye held out his arms, shaking. He hated to be lying there, naked, atop the urine stains and grime from the bottoms of countless feet.

Dirty bathroom floor, dirty alley. Not much different, are they?

The baton dragged lower, raking over the skin of his back until it was nudging between his cheeks, pressing right at his hole.

"Gonna behave for me, little piggy?" Ecker asked with a psychotically lighthearted tone. "Or do I need to give you more... motivation? Maybe stick you on a spit to roast?" The baton pushed harder, trying to enter him. Jaye grunted and fought to stay still, to not give Ecker a reason to beat him again.

"Please don't," he begged quietly.

"I should get one of my friends over here; do you from the front with his stick at the same time...." The pressure from the baton increased.

He grunted, then cried, "I'll behave!"

"Are you my piggy?"

"Yes!"

"How's that feel?" The end of the baton twisted, corkscrewing into him. "You like that?"

"No!"

Stuck it right in, just like you wanted me to, didn't I?

"Please take it out!"

You like to get poked?

"I don't! I don't like it!"

You know what we do to monsters? Little faggoty ones like you?

"Fuck you! You're dead!"

"What was that?" Ecker asked, the warning plain in his tone.

Jaye made a startled noise, his whole body trembling violently as the baton pushed past his rim.

Jaye realized he'd responded to Burt aloud. Hating the dry, bruising, burning ache of the baton prying him open, and petrified of what was happening, he pleaded, "I'm sorry! I'm sorry, okay! I'll cooperate, I swear!"

"Gonna get up and bend over for me?"

Oh god.

"Yes."

Too slowly, the baton withdrew again. His hole was sore; his faith in his ability to endure what was about to happen shattered.

"Get up. Hands on the wall. Spread those legs wide."

Ecker ran his hands down Jaye's sides, down the outsides of his bare legs, then up the insides. He stopped when he got to Jaye's genitals, and those long, clammy, spindly fingers toyed with his dick and balls. Behind him, Ecker was breathing hard.

"You know how I want ya, piggy."

He fuckin' loves it.

Jaye fought not to speak, the voices of Burt and Earl as loud and clear as the voice of Ecker from right behind Jaye as he bent over and grabbed behind his knees again.

When Ecker drove two fingers up Jaye's hole, hooking them in there, Jaye grimaced, writhing a little and heard Earl say: *Look at him dance!*

It went on and on. He was impaled and raped like that for hours, days. Ecker gave him long, complete penetrating strokes, during which Jaye quivered and whined. Ecker's free hand kept fiddling with Jaye's dick and balls, sending squirming signals of pure revulsion wriggling into Jaye's gut. Burt said: *You like that? You like to get poked?* And Jaye shook his head in reply.

He began having trouble keeping track of what was happening. Reality was dissolving at the edges, slipping from his grasp. Was Burt really there? Was Ecker? Was any of it even real? Was he back in his cell, imagining the whole thing? He didn't know if he was hallucinating or not.

There was touching, fondling, fingering. The fingers twisting in his guts felt as real as the ones tugging on the end of his dick and poking up his ass.

He heard two voices at once. One was Ecker saying: *You like that? You like to get poked? You know what we do to monsters?* The other was Burt asking: *Are you my piggy?*

Did he imagine both? Neither?

"Help me," Jaye breathed, shivering.

The index finger of Ecker's left hand found Jaye's mouth and dove down his gullet.

"Gonna squeal, piggy?"

Gonna cry?

We know you like it, Johnny. You piggy. Piggy whore.

"How's that feel?"

You asked for it, piggy. You earned it.

The voices multiplied, blended. Jaye was surrounded. It didn't matter that it was just Ecker there. Not when Ecker was inside Jaye's head as well as inside his body, poking around in both places, leaving mental scars when the physical hurts had long healed over.

Groaning sickly, Jaye began to battle with the taunting of his ghosts much more than the violations of his body. He was coming apart. Losing it. Knowing some of it wasn't real, but not able to tell which parts, was terrifying. Fingers were everywhere, tugging at the skin of his sac, thrusting up his rectum, pulling at his internal organs, peeling back his skin, and rubbing his tongue. It was all just a tangle of sensory information he didn't want to process.

It overtook everything.

It didn't end. It faded away.

At some point, he had blacked out. A mental switch had flicked, shutting out the lights even while, physically, he'd carried on.

"Johnny? Johnny, man, you okay?"

He came to a little.

He was on his knees in front of the toilet, the stall door open. He was quietly murmuring, "Help me," over and over again. His hand was on the toilet's handle and he just kept flushing. The water ran and ran and ran. Grunting thickly, shaking violently, covered in a film of cold sweat from forehead to ankles, and a string of saliva extending down from his lower lip, he understood Hax was behind him, not Ecker, but he didn't know how to move or stop.

Hax pulled Jaye to his feet and handed him his discarded towel. When Jaye just stood there, holding the towel and wearing a blank expression, Hax carefully tugged the towel out of Jaye's loose grip, then wrapped it around Jaye's slim hips. Hax tucked the towel in and patted Jaye gently on his shoulder.

"I'll kill him, Hax," Jaye said softly. "I'll fucking kill him. I just need to figure out how."

"Come on, kid. Let's get you out of here." Hax stayed at Jaye's side all the way back to his cell.

Us and them, Jaye thought. *We all picked sides. Cops, lawyers, guards, and doctors on one. Everyone in here who's been fucked over on the other. Now we just need to fight the war.*

Standing in his cell, he looked at his toothbrush over by the sink, and thought, maybe, if he snapped off the end, filed it down to a point... maybe it'd be just what he needed to be ready for the next battle he knew was coming, sooner than later.

Chapter 17
Mental Health Concerns

Because Jaye generally looked like death warmed over and had a couple of fairly public episodes with his ghosts, he was sent to meet with the Unit 4 Psychologist, Peter O'Neill. The idea was for Jaye to talk things out and explain what was bothering him.

It didn't really work out like that. There wasn't much talking Jaye was willing to do.

"Is anyone giving you a hard time?" O'Neill had asked. He was sitting behind his desk, the two of them shut up inside the Mental Health office. The windows were larger in there, though covered with dusty, half-opened blinds discolored with age. Some of the thin plastic slats were snapped off at the end. The view of the blue sky and green trees beyond the room, beyond even the tall fence topped with barbed wire as well, was interrupted in horizontal slices. Jaye stared at it, piecing the shattered view back together, trying to mentally escape the dingy, musty-smelling room. O'Neill had a few small plants on the edge of his desk, but they were wilted. It didn't say much for his ability to even keep simpler living things alive.

Jaye shrugged, slouched down in his chair. He'd lost about fifteen pounds in three weeks, and he'd been skinny to start with. Not only was he wasting away almost to skin and bones, he exercised in his cell as often as he could, wasn't eating much of anything, and wasn't sleeping either. Basically, he was a mess. He knew it.

The ghosts were getting louder, bothering him when there wasn't even anything triggering him. They came out of nowhere. Touching. Whispering. Promising.

"Are you being targeted by anyone?"

Jaye kept a straight face and scratched at the inside of his wrist. Something was tickling it. He couldn't make it stop. When his hand began to shake, he folded his arms instead.

O'Neill glanced down at the report on his desk — a sheet of white paper atop a small stack which lay inside an opened blue paper folder — then back up at Jaye. O'Neill was an older guy who had a grandfatherly sort of look to him. His thinning hair stood up a little. His ears were big and droopy; the skin around his eyes crinkled and sagged. He wore thick black glasses, had a small pot belly and a set of man-boobs, but there was worry in his eyes. Maybe even hints of kindness and intelligence. It was easy to imagine little kids running at him with their arms opened, laughing and happy. It only made Jaye more suspicious and wary. There hadn't been many reliable grandfatherly figures in his life.

"You were screaming in the cafeteria, repeatedly slamming a tray against a wall," O'Neill said leadingly, like he was checking to see whether Jaye had any memory of the incident. "When the guards moved to restrain you, you began hitting your head against the wall instead."

Jaye smiled coldly. "Yeah, I remember." His souvenirs from that little stunt were a nasty bruise and scrapes on his temple, along with a steady throbbing headache that was doing a surprisingly good job of shutting up the invisible assholes in his brain. He glanced back at the chopped blue and green view, the brightness out there drawing him in.

O'Neill flipped a few pages over. With a steady look, he said, "You've also been overheard talking to yourself. Angrily."

Jaye laughed and shook his head. A chocolate curling tendril fell over his eye. He left it there, hiding behind it. "Yeah, I can be an intolerable bitch sometimes."

"I'm concerned about your mental health, Mr. Larson," O'Neill said with some tenderness, which Jaye resented. "I'd like to send you for further evaluation by our medical staff, and we'll be prescribing you something to help with regulating your anxiety."

"Okay. Whatever. I don't think it'll help, but I'll give it a shot."

"If anyone harms or hurts you, I want you to report it right away, or come to me directly."

"Why?" Jaye asked with a sly upward glance through the curtain of his hair. "You get off on the juicy details of teenagers getting raped?"

"Is that what happened to you?" O'Neill asked, his crinkled eyes widening as he effectively pounced on the possible confession.

"No," Jaye said curtly, dropping his gaze again.

"There's no need to lie to protect anyone. If you can give me just a little bit of information—"

"I said no!" Jaye shouted. "Never happened."

"Never happened," O'Neill echoed, sitting back with a loud creak in his chair. "Is that what Jones told you to say?"

Jaye breathed out a cynical little chuckle. "Cash never did nothing to me. He's a good guy. He's the best guy in here I know."

"Really?" O'Neill replied with disbelief dripping from the word. "Mr. Larson, while you are staying with us, we are charged with keeping you safe. I want to help you, but I can't do that if you can't give me something to work with here. You're the youngest person in our facility and I have more than enough here," he tapped the stack of untidy papers in front of him with a thick index finger, "to be concerned."

As soon as Jaye saw O'Neill's finger jab the official record of Jaye's behavioral issues, the touching started again. Hands without substance groped between his legs, wriggled up his rectum and rubbed the back of his tongue, sliding deeply into his throat.

Where'd you hide it, Johnny? We know it's here somewhere.

You like that, piggy?

Gonna slice you open.

Wanna watch?

Gonna cry?

"Mr. Larson!"

"I didn't take anything!" Jaye shouted hoarsely, his voice cracking with strain. "I didn't do anything!"

"Mr. Larson! Look at me! Right now!"

Curled up tightly in his chair, hands over his head as if to shield it and breathing hard, Jaye made the effort to relax enough to make eye contact. It took a solid minute or two before he was able to manage it.

"Whatever is behind all of this," O'Neill said severely, "you have a duty to report it. I can't do anything for you if I don't know what's wrong."

Jaye just stared back at him.

When nothing more was said, O'Neill picked up his phone and made a call. "Yeah, I need someone to get in here and escort Mr. Larson to Health Services. Thank you."

Jaye wasn't sure what the orange pills were in the little cup they gave him in Health Services, but after he swallowed them down, he relaxed quite a lot. They told him he would need to visit the medication line each morning at six thirty for the foreseeable future to receive his allotted dosage.

Dazed, shuffling along, his muscles increasingly lax, his head stuffed with cotton wool, he followed the guard chaperoning him on the trip back to Unit 4. Jaye moved only where he was pointed, not at all really caring where he was. Sounds were reaching his ears more slowly. His body felt heavier, steps harder to take. Instead, he shuffled and squinted against the sound lag. As he passed people, he saw their lips moving, but the words took a few seconds to crawl through the air, like the ghosts had snagged the ends and were pulling them back.

Nearby, someone was yelling. "What the fuck is this? Hey! Hey, what the fuck did you do to him?"

"Easy, Mr. Jones," the guard retorted. "You don't want to return to where you just came from, do you?"

It was all happening someplace else, behind a thick, fogged-over screen, outside of the fuzziness surrounding Jaye. His cuffs were removed. He saw there was a familiar looking cot right in front of him. He sat on it, his knees giving way, tumbling him down, and let his too-heavy hands hang down between his knees.

There was movement around him, trying to snag his gaze and failing. He was distantly aware of more talking he didn't take the effort to comprehend, the words running into each other, overlapping.

Someone roughly grabbed his face, tilting it upward. The lights' glare hit his eyes and made him need to close them. It was far too bright.

"What'd they fucking give you, Johnny? I've seen roadkill in better shape than you right now. What the hell happened to your head? Why are you so fucking skinny? Hey! Snap out of it!"

"Hands off of Larson, Jones! That's your last warning!"

The touching stopped. The noises in general dulled even more, like he was behind several screens instead of only one. The cot grew more comfortable, swallowing him up. His body grew steadily heavier until he let it collapse sideways onto the bed.

For a while, he slept dreamlessly.

Each time Jaye surfaced, the light in the cell was different. The noise inside and outside of his head was nothing but a steady hum that kept lulling him back to sleep. Before he knew it, it was morning again. They were waking everyone up by the time anything started to make sense.

The foggy feeling remained, but it was easier to deal with than before. The last day had been a wash of nothingness, ever since they'd taken him to see O'Neill.

He figured the drugs were some sort of sedative or downer. They could be anti-psychotic pills for all he knew. He didn't really give a shit. In fact, he was sure they'd explained the medication to him at Health Services. Maybe it had been something like Florazine. He couldn't remember. Listening hadn't exactly been a priority.

Jaye got up to use the toilet and sat there, looking at Cash sitting on the top bunk, staring at him.

"You're not here," Jaye said softly.

"The fuck I'm not."

Cash hopped down and grabbed Jaye by the chin.

"Doesn't prove anything. The ghosts touch me too and they're not real either." Jaye finished up and flushed. He washed his hands while, in the mirror above the sink, the ghost of Cash stared at the back of his head.

"Why do you have ghosts?"

"I don't know. Ask them."

"Who did this? Who do I gotta fucking hurt to make this right?"

Jaye didn't answer, even to tell a ghost. Ratting would only amp up the torture the next time Ecker came around, and he would come around sooner or later.

"They told me Ecker's been stopping by regularly."

Who's been talking to a ghost? Other ghosts?

"You've got ghosts too? How's that possible?"

Jaye kept his back to Cash's ghost. He didn't like seeing things that weren't there.

"I got a crew," the ghost explained, sounding half aggravated and half plain old freaked out. "They're as fucking real as you'd want. What'd they do to you, kid? Why'd they dope you up?"

"I freaked out in the caf and in O'Neill's office. Knocked my head against the wall a few times, trying to make the ghosts shut up. I don't want to hear their shit anymore. I don't want them touching me, either. They can't tell me what to do. I'll fight back. I swear I will. Just have to figure out how. I'm not theirs. I'm not their...."

Softly, from behind him, Cash's voice asked, "Their what?"

"...piggy."

A hand gripped Jaye's shoulder. He spun and his fist swung around, instinctively. There had been no fear to keep his reflexes contained and his body pinned down. The drugs would have slowed him if they were still freshly impacting his system, but they were fading out. All he knew was the need to make the touching stop, and he was willing to fight to make it happen.

His punch connected with the side of Cash's jaw.

"Don't touch me!" Jaye screamed frantically, trying to punch again, but Cash backed him to the wall and clapped a palm over Jaye's mouth to hold in his shouts. Without much effort at all, Cash held him still, completely immobilized.

Panting, adrenaline dumping into his system, blasting more of his fog away, Jaye finally, slowly, realized it really was Cash standing there. It wasn't just in his head.

Cash gave him time, let him see and get it through his thick skull. The fight was slow to fade, though, so Cash kept him pinned a while longer, even after Jaye stopped trying to cry out and was just breathing hard against Cash's hand, his eyes too wide.

"You with me now?" Cash asked calmly.

Jaye nodded.

"You still think I'm a ghost?"

A pause of consideration, then a shake of his head. That's when the relief hit, strong enough to flood Jaye with desperately craved, heartwarming reassurance that he could relax, at last.

Cash was gripping Jaye's jaw with one hand to silence him. His other arm was thrown across Jaye's chest. Jaye's hands gripped that arm, hard. The relief came in waves, crashing into him. He melted into the wall behind him, welcoming the pressure of Cash's solid body against him, even if it hurt.

"I'm gonna let go," Cash warned.

Jaye nodded.

The hand released his jaw. He stayed quiet.

"Ecker fucking put his hands on you?"

A nod.

"Searching you for shit?"

Jaye's gaze skittered away. Cash just yanked his focus back, getting right up in his face.

"Has he fucked you?"

Four little words, but they were so angry. There was murder and blood and screaming underneath the glossy surface of them, and that scared Jaye enough to hesitate.

"Talk," Cash ordered. Simple. Direct. Ruthless.

It was impossible not to be scared, even though, rationally, Jaye knew Cash wouldn't harm him. Cash was so much bigger, so much stronger and meaner. If he had fuel to feed his rage, anything could happen. Cash had killed people, maimed people. He'd done shit Jaye never wanted to even have to imagine.

Speaking low enough for the words to be barely audible, Jaye said, "Used his... baton. Inside me. Just a little. And fingers. Really long f— Down my throat. Up my... Up my ass. Been puking so much, I don't want to ever see food again."

The expression on Cash's face was chilling, so Jaye tried to look away. He really did. He felt his bladder let go, but thankfully he'd just emptied it, so nothing came out. Cash wasn't just going to kill Ecker, he was going to fucking dissect the guy, pulling him apart while he was still conscious like Jaye's attackers had tried to do to him once upon a time.

Cash didn't say a word about what he thought of what Jaye had just said. He didn't promise or imply anything. He didn't have to. It was all right there in his cold, dead-eyed stare.

"You hearing ghosts right now?" Cash asked after a long moment.

Jaye shook his head.

"Good. Tell me if you do. I'll get rid of them."

A shrill buzz shook the air, signaling that they all needed to line up for the showers.

"You're gonna eat," Cash told him. "I don't care if you don't want to. That's what you worry about now — the only thing you worry about. Eating."

Jaye nodded, wanting to kiss Cash, to curl up at his feet and lie there, safe and protected. Since he couldn't, as he got his things for the shower and went to stand where he was supposed to, he internalized the good feelings as fuel for his courage and more reasons to believe he could fight his way through this. With Cash there, looking out, anything was possible.

All day he'd seen it. Playing the part of a ghost, himself, Jaye stayed silent but kept watch always, for everything and anything. Cash had talked to the whole crew, in small groups, here and there. The message was simple: Ecker was a target. He wasn't to be allowed to get Jaye alone, if anyone could do anything to prevent it. They were charged with talking to their contacts on the outside, to look into Ecker's personal life. See if he cared about anyone they could use as leverage.

The crew didn't seem to resent it. Instead, they were fired up with the chance to focus all of their collective willingness to fuck shit up at one particular guy. One demented, corrupt guard.

It helped clear Jaye's head in a big way.

When he was given that day's dose of meds, he downed them happily. The fog settled, but it was calming and he let go knowing he was safe now that Cash had returned. Having food in his stomach this time also helped lessen the severity of the side effects. Sure, Ecker would still come around, but he'd get his. It might not happen right away, but it would happen. Just like how Rico's leg had snapped. It was unavoidable now. So, Jaye would put up with whatever pathetic shit Ecker had to dish out. When he got his, there was no question it would be so much worse.

That night, after lights out, when Cash didn't come to Jaye's cot for sex like he'd always done without fail, Jaye acted. He had to.

Waiting until after the guard on patrol cleared their cell, Jaye somewhat groggily moved up to Cash's bed and swung a leg over him, straddling him.

There was a bemused, patient expression on Cash's gnarled face, but his hands gently clasped Jaye's thighs, rubbing a little. Leaning down close so it looked like there was only one person in the bed rather than two, he worked Cash's pants down and freed his dick. Stroking the thick, hot column, Jaye let Cash undress him, too. Moaning softly, grinding against Cash's thigh, Jaye was hugely turned on before they'd even really started.

"Feel so good," Jaye whispered heatedly. "Missed you so much."

With the meds keeping what was left of his anxiety in check, he felt closer to Cash than ever, with nothing holding in his pure, honest reactions. With the contraband lube, hidden inside a tear in his mattress, Cash slicked his hand and worked Jaye open.

"Mm, yeah," Jaye frowned, biting his lip. "Thank you."

Jaye humped Cash's fingers, his brow furrowed, and his little bounces greedy and wanton. The more he put on a show of just how much he really wanted it, the more it darkened Cash's expression, filling it with a crackling, electric storm of lust.

When he couldn't wait anymore, Jaye brushed his lips over the upper edge of Cash's stubble-covered jaw, then his ear and begged, "Please? Do it. Fuck me. Make me yours."

He reached behind himself and aligned Cash's cock. Sinking down onto it with a sigh, Jaye shuddered with pleasure. Cash's hands were on him, pawing, squeezing, and rough in the ways only real, intense and mutual attraction allowed. He pulled at Jaye's hair, caressed his gasping, parted lips, tugged his cock and kneaded his ass. The sex was mind-blowingly good. Jaye clenched each time he rocked forward and Cash's dick tugged out, then pushed back down onto him with needy little groans.

Jaye came first, with a trembling whimper that had Cash biting at

Jaye's lip and slipping him his tongue with a moan of his own.

Moving on Cash with a steady push and pull, still riding the high, Jaye nuzzled Cash's neck and vowed, "Yours. Always."

"Anyone touches you, anyone harms you in any way, *they pay*," Cash told him.

"Fuck yes," Jaye moaned, riding him harder, never wanting it to end.

Chapter 18
Business Transaction

"Look, I might have found a way to get rid of Ecker for a while."

They were outside, leaning against the fence in the recreation yard. The Disciples formed a loose, wide ring around them, keeping everyone else away. It was an overcast day, the leaden, grey clouds weighed down and threatening, but Jaye cherished any outdoor time he got. The brisk, fresh air against his skin was even better than sunshine. That day the wind was really blowing, like a storm was coming. It tossed his long hair back through the fence and away from his face. It felt like parts of him were breaking free of that little concrete yard, wandering off like his ghosts could.

It was hard to believe that more than half a year had passed already. Factoring in the time he'd spent in the hospital, then awaiting trial and sentencing, it was almost a year since the night Burt Mc-Curdy and Earl Humphrey had attacked Jaye. Soon, Jaye was going to be twenty years old. His days as a teenager were numbered. It was easier to count those than the days left on his sentence. There was still too much time remaining for it to be at all comforting to do the math.

He resolved that the next time he got hold of his lawyer he was going to ask about his grandfather. It would be good to at least have someone in mind to visit once he was free again. It would be the little light of hope, shining in the distance.

"No shit?" Jaye replied, not paying one hundred percent attention. The meds had been doing a pretty good job of keeping him calm and getting rid of the ghosts that always tagged along with his fluctuating anxiety levels. But they also made it hard to concentrate on anything. His thoughts skipped around, bopping along on a bunch of topics without latching on strongly or for more than a moment. And Ecker was one topic he automatically veered away from, fast. "You're good at that, aren't you? Figuring stuff out. Gettin' it done. Like me," he grinned. "You do me right all the time."

Ecker was an unsolvable problem. Wasting time worrying about something Jaye couldn't change helped nothing.

"No shit," Cash echoed, putting a little more force in it than Jaye had, like he could tell Jaye was drifting again.

Jaye glanced over at his benefactor and possessor. The natural light was much kinder to Cash than the fluorescents. Jaye was usually privately glad they typically had sex in the dark, because then Cash could be anyone Jaye wanted to picture instead of a ruthless killer who'd been chewed up and spit out more than a couple of times. "You look better outside. Less scary. Guess you'll always be scary on the inside, though."

His intense gaze boring sharply into Jaye, Cash said, "It's not a permanent solution, but it'll do."

"Well, what is it?" Jaye asked, taking the bait even though he wanted to just lean back and find pictures in the thick, blue-grey clouds shifting above them. "Not that I'm picky. Anything that gets that wormy fucker offa me works."

Ecker had barely come around since Cash had returned, but Jaye knew it was only a matter of time. Things would pick up again. He wasn't stupid.

"Dorrance says he can get Ecker transferred for a few months. Some probationary thing. Says he could come forward as a witness to Ecker roughing up some of my guys. It wouldn't get tied to you at all, and Ecker gives our crew more shit than anyone anyway. The suits would buy it. Ecker would get a warning and be separated from prisoners for a solid three to six months."

That snagged Jaye's attention, hard. Smiling hugely with surprise, he said, "Are you fucking kidding me? That's amazing! Man... you're so good to me, boss. I'll make it up to you, okay? I swear. It's just... I never thought anyone would ever wanna take care of me again the way you do. Everyone else left me to die, but not you. You keep coming through, no matter what. Guess that's why they made you the boss, huh?"

Cash smiled to see Jaye happy and then glanced away. "He'd need to be compensated. Dorrance."

"Fine," Jaye said automatically.

"You sure? 'Cause you're the payment."

Faintly, the memories of his gang bang in administrative-segregation stirred. He remembered what it had felt like to be cuffed and bent over a metal table to be raped by a roomful of men. His terror and helplessness as Dorrance in particular had force-fucked him was impossible to forget, but it had been a one-time deal. Dorrance had never come after Jaye again afterward. At least there was a measure of control to what had happened in that isolation cell. It had all only happened at Cash's insistence. Ecker's attacks had no form of control to them. They were wild, cruel and never-ending. If he had to choose between his monsters, he'd pick Dorrance over Ecker in a heartbeat.

A couple of the guys — Wolf and Jinx — glanced over for just a second. Jaye tried not to care if they heard, and mostly he didn't. Words were nothing compared to deeds. He had to trust Cash's crew with some information. They already got a free sex show on a regular basis. Since Cash had been back, he'd fucked Jaye in the showers a few times, with everyone around, and once in the corner of the Unit 4 common area while a guy named Sanchez enjoyed a front row seat. That had been payment, too, for something Jaye knew nothing about. But Cash had let Sanchez pet Jaye's hair and ass while Cash fucked Jaye hard and held him down. No big deal.

"Already been the payment once, haven't I? Got the nightmares to prove it. Scratched me up good too, but those faded. What's he want?" Jaye asked, drifting again, paying more attention to the clouds than anything else. "Another video? Him and his buddies take their turns, watch me cry on camera some more?"

The meds would help, at least. They'd keep him floating.

"No. This time he wants access. Private time. With you. Guess he's taken a liking."

It made sense. All of those times when Cash publicly displayed their arrangement, treating Jaye like a filthy whore to boost his own reputation; it was Dorrance who watched out. That meant he wasn't just making sure none of the other guards gave them shit, he was also getting to enjoy the show himself. Now he wanted to get his hands on

Cash's prize, alone. No buddies. No cameras. No Cash.

"Doesn't want anything freaky, from what he told me. Just sex."

"Yeah right. Does that mean he's not gonna spank me this time?"

"If he does, you say thank you and beg him for more. I need you to make it special. Make him think you love every second you've got with him. Far as you're concerned, he's the best fuck you've ever had in your life. You do that, Ecker's gone. For now."

"Fine. No problem. Got some good fuckin' experience with role-play, don't I?" Jaye answered without really thinking about it. He was already somewhere else, somewhere better, where he wasn't just meat that got passed around for guys to poke at.

"You sure?"

"I'm sure. Wouldn't have lost my goddamned mind if not for that motherfuckin' Ecker. He needs to go. Even just for a while. I'm in."

It took about a week before Dorrance called in his payment. The day before Jaye's twentieth birthday, Dorrance pulled him into a storage closet when he was supposed to be escorting Jaye back from an appointment with O'Neill, the Unit 4 headshrinker. The whole thing was kind of hilarious. It seemed the day was going to consist of therapy, transactional sex, then a happy birthday for Johnny, hopefully, if Dorrance came through. All in all, if everything went smoothly, it would be a massive improvement on Jaye's last birthday.

The storage closet's door closed softly behind them. It was barely big enough in there for both of them, the walls lined with metal shelves holding cleaning and office supplies. The only light was what filtered through the narrow window in the door. Dorrance wore an eager, creepy sort of grin.

This was business, nothing more. Jaye knew it. Dorrance wanted payment up front, before he put his neck on the line for Cash's whore.

The close quarters and privacy gave Jaye a chance to get a good look at Dorrance. He was pretty normal looking, with dark hair buzzed short, a square jaw, brown eyes, and about thirty five years old. Basically, he was nothing special, but nothing too horrifying either. Maybe without the guard uniform, he'd look more attractive, and more human. It was hard for Jaye to see past an exterior that had become so off-putting.

Jaye had gotten suspicious that he would likely find himself alone with Dorrance at some point that day, just from the way he'd caught Dorrance looking at him in the showers that morning, blatantly palming himself while Jaye soaped up his body. So Jaye had skipped most of his meals, knowing the meds would hit him harder on an empty stomach.

The whole encounter was likely to be much easier and enjoyable if things were fuzzy at the edges.

He was flying pretty high when he stepped up to Dorrance, laying a hand on the guard's chest. Jaye smiled, biting shyly at the edge of his lower lip.

"You want me?"

"Sure do," Dorrance grinned, palming Jaye's ass and giving it a hard squeeze. With his other hand, Dorrance grabbed hold of Jaye's jaw, giving the side of his face a firm caress. "Never saw a guy pretty as you. If I hadn't seen your cock so many times, I'd have sworn you had a pussy."

It was kind of pathetic how freely some guys, like Dorrance, wore their lust out where everyone could see it. Jaye couldn't imagine drooling so publicly over anyone he didn't have a contractual agreement with. Stroking an ego in those circumstances was one thing. It was excusable. But to make a fool of yourself by getting hot and bothered over someone was something he didn't think he was capable of doing anymore. Sure, once he had been prone to behaving that way, before he'd died. But this was another life, a different incarnation, and this one held only pity for suckers like Dorrance.

Dorrance swept Jaye's hair over his shoulder, then began to play with the curling ends.

"I don't need a pussy to fuck you better than anyone else in your whole life," Jaye promised. He leaned in to kiss the side of Dorrance's neck.

Jaye's clothes were pulled off or pushed down, along with his boxers. When Dorrance began rubbing Jaye's balls, invisible fingers started to claw at Jaye's brain. All of his bad-touch alarms wanted to blare, but the meds took over first, melting the panic away shortly after it had begun to manifest.

Not even flinching, but stilling and breathing hard, Jaye allowed the touches. He didn't struggle or show any sign he didn't welcome them. Like Cash had warned him earlier, it was important for Jaye to sell the act. All the motivation Jaye needed was to think of months on end without Ecker coming for him.

At least Dorrance could be tempted and played to Jaye's advantage. Ecker only wanted Jaye to suffer.

"You wanna fuck my mouth?" he asked hopefully. "I can deep throat you, no problem."

"Not today. Only got one thing on my mind."

He manhandled Jaye around. Grabbing him by the back of the neck and the hip, Dorrance bent Jaye over sharply at the waist. Jaye braced himself against the closet's shelves, gripping one that held stacks of worn, fraying towels that looked like they had been washed a couple billion times. Behind him, a condom wrapper ripped open. Jaye sighed with a dazed sort of relief that at least he wouldn't be left with come in his ass again.

"Prettiest come rag I ever did see," Dorrance said breathlessly as he lined up and pressed the head of his dick between Jaye's cheeks. There hadn't been any sort of prep or lube, and Cash hadn't touched Jaye at all that day, so it hurt almost right away as Dorrance tried to enter him. Jaye made a pained grunt, grabbing so tightly onto the shelf that the metal edge dug into his hands. He tried to steady himself, gritting his teeth and breathing through the low flare of intimate pain. By Jaye's ear, Dorrance said, "Oh, come on. You can take it, Johnny. I'm not packing what Cash is, and he reams you out nightly, like clockwork. You know how many times I've spanked it, listening to him plow this tight little ass of yours?"

Dorrance pushed sharply, ignoring Jaye's startled, small cry. The head was through Jaye's outer ring. Dorrance eased up, not pushing as hard and mostly just letting Jaye's ass pull him in the rest of the way.

"Mmm, yeah, that's it. That's what I've been wanting to feel again."

Gasping, shuddering, Jaye knew how sore he'd be when this was through. He tried to stay loose, but it didn't do much good. The dry friction burned, making him wince. Shifting his stance wider didn't help either, his ass gripped tightly around Dorrance's cock.

It was awful, but then Jaye remembered Ecker.

Ecker was worse. A lot worse.

After Dorrance spat on his hand, pulled slightly out, then rubbed the fluid on his shaft, Jaye was relieved. He started to move on Dorrance, riding his dick with shallow movements. Dorrance was right, his dick wasn't so big after all. Once the movement stretched Jaye out a little, Dorrance was sliding easy, and the hurt eased.

Jaye let out what he hoped was a slutty moan, bouncing back onto the cock, tossing his long hair over a shoulder. Dorrance played with the ends again, twirling them around his fingers, breathing heavily.

He reached for Jaye's dick. When he found Jaye half-hard, Dorrance went for it, jerking him off, and that made the sex even better.

Soon, Jaye was humping Dorrance's fist and taking the cock easily, with soft gasps.

"Yeah, you fuckin' like that, don't you, Johnny? You fuckin' whore. You fuckin' come rag."

Jaye hummed, blocking out the words, letting the drugs unravel his thoughts and awareness, taking him someplace else.

A week later, it had all gone down. Kett and Tug had beaten the shit out of each other. The injuries were nothing permanent and there were no broken bones, but it was plenty for Health Services to deal with, afterward. The fight happened on Ecker's watch even though, technically, Ecker had been nowhere nearby. Ecker had been at one end of the recreation yard, Kett, Tug and the rest of the Disciples at the other, blocking the view. Dorrance came forward with witness testimony that he'd seen Ecker throwing kicks and punches, but that Ecker had taken off as soon as he saw Dorrance coming to stop him from savagely beating the inmates.

Ecker was given paid leave, as Dorrance had promised. It was done quietly, with no fanfare. They only knew about it because Dorrance told them. The warden had also said that after Ecker's leave was up, he would be moved to another post where he didn't have as much direct contact with the prisoners.

Jaye was riding high.

Though a week late, it was the best birthday present he'd ever received. The dread which had burdened him for so long was lifted. With Ecker out of the way, everyday life in the prison wasn't nearly as unbearable or intimidating.

Day by day, Jaye started feeling much more confident. The fear melted back so far, he thought soon he could talk to O'Neill about maybe going off of the meds, or at least cutting back on his dosage.

Soon after Ecker had disappeared, Dorrance came around again.

Jaye was ready this time. He'd been fingering himself during bathroom breaks, just in case, and regularly used some of Cash's stash of lube, too.

As soon as Dorrance stripped Jaye's clothes off and bent him over, he slid right into Jaye with a satisfied moan. That afternoon, Dorrance enjoyed himself with Jaye so much, he stayed buried and played with Jaye's dick until he was ready for round two.

They both walked away feeling quite satisfied.

Chapter 19
Good Times, Bad Times

It was the start of some good times for Jaye. Ecker was out of Jaye's hair. Business with the Disciples was good, so Cash was always smiling and in high spirits. Cash never included Jaye in his business transactions with smuggling and dealing, but that was just how Jaye liked it. He didn't mind when Cash would tell him to get lost if he needed to work things out with a client. Jaye knew he was better off in the dark. The Disciples' shit wasn't his problem, and that was just fine. Jaye's only problem was keeping Cash happy and life was doing half the job for him. When Cash came to Jaye in those days after Ecker was given leave, Jaye was always hard and plenty sweet. He said his thank yous and gave Cash anything he could want.

Their worries were few and far between, especially with Dorrance watching their backs. If business was good for Cash, then business was good for Dorrance. It was win-win. And really, all Jaye cared about was being able to relax and coast through the days. Each one that ticked by got him closer to his release date.

Jaye could see the respect even guys in other crews had for Cash. Since Cash was the pipeline to things they needed, they kept hands off. No one gave him shit, which meant no one gave Jaye shit. He was Johnny, Cash's boy, always by his side.

Walking through the common areas, eating in the dining hall, even when using the showers, there were no more cat calls or threats, like there had been before. Other inmates nodded when they caught Jaye's eye, in a sign of respect. Sure, they still looked him up and down, but Jaye wasn't stupid. He knew his place. He was a piece of ass. That was his value.

At least he *had* value.

The most important thing was that the others wouldn't touch him, because if they did, they brought down Cash's full wrath upon their heads.

There was a lot Jaye had gotten used to, since he'd arrived at FCI Sheridan. When walking the line in the dining hall waiting to collect his tray of watery, bland grub, he accepted the platter of gray meat and thin potatoes with a tight-lipped smile from Perez, who ran with the Latin Lords. Perez nodded back, his gaze flicking over to Jaye's inked tear, then down the front of his body. Jaye let his smile grow, twisting up the corner of his mouth, and kept moving.

It was just one more way he was measured up, his worth easily accountable in the grand scheme of things.

The tension never really left. Tray in hand, Jaye walked, limping only slightly, over to the table where most of the Disciples sat. They filled the pair of benches in two long rows. Everyone was in the same regulation clothing. It was their ink, scars, and haircuts which distinguished them. They were just a bunch of rough-looking thugs who'd done bad shit and had it catch up with them. Jaye didn't feel like he belonged. Not completely.

As he walked up to the empty spot beside Cash, Jaye felt many sets of eyes on him — his long, curly hair, his full lips, and his ass — knowing they were imagining him sucking or taking cock to earn his seat at their table.

It wasn't like he was part of the crew, or the pipeline of getting cigarettes and drugs out there into people's hands. He wasn't muscle and he wasn't an earner. He was just a stupid piece of ass who kept the boss in good spirits.

So he prayed his thanks that he had Cash, counting his blessings and his days.

"Lookin' good, Johnny," Cash grinned, slapping Jaye's ass as he set his tray down on the table.

Jaye stepped over the bench and sat as Ro asked Cash, "You seen Tio and his boys?"

"Why?" Cash lost his grin and stared back at Ro. Jaye glanced over a shoulder at the Warlords crew. Tio, sitting next to a huge linebacker-sized guy named Smalls, was there, boring bloody holes in the back of Cash's head with his stare alone. There was a lot of ill will in the intensity of that stare. It gave Jaye a bad feeling which didn't fade but only caused intangible fingers to caress lightly over his skin beneath his clothes.

"Ever since Ecker shipped out, been something off there. Just sayin'. Don't know why."

"Maybe they had a deal. He was doing them favors," Hax guessed.

"It would make sense," Ro nodded, giving Cash a telling look. "Just watch your back, boss. Christ knows what those shitheads are up to."

The ghosts tugged at the ends of Jaye's hair, so he swept it over his shoulder and cleared his throat. The meds were too strong for the ghosts to really grab hold of him, and their voices were too muted to make out. He knew they were there though, and that was bad enough.

The moment breathed, then Jaye saw Cash glance back at Tio and return that icy stare of his. Cash was grinning a little, but there was nothing good in it. Just seeing a look that threatening on Cash's face made the ghosts tickle Jaye's balls a little harder.

More warning. More unease.

Jaye murmured under his breath, hopefully too low for the others to hear, "Hands off, you fuckers. You're not there. Hands off."

"You okay, Johnny?"

Jaye looked up at Cash and put on his most convincing smile. "Sure, boss."

Cash palmed Jaye's ass, giving it a squeeze and a pat. Voices in Jaye's head whispered from far away.

You like that, you whore? Everyone knows, piggy. Everyone sees. All you are is warm meat to fuck. A hole to stick a cock in. You're not even human. You're an it.

Jaye closed his eyes and focused on Cash's touch. It was more real than the voices, and more reassuring than the stares he wouldn't be able to escape until he paroled.

When he opened his eyes again, the voices were gone. He felt steadier. But he happened to lock eyes with Princess, who was really Vargas, the prison wife of Montez. Montez was the lead motherfucker of the Latin Lords crew. Princess was skinny, small, and young, but he wasn't pretty, like Jaye, so he wore contraband lipstick, and tied his shirt up like a girl would. Princess was a few tables away and wearing a dead, hollow sort of expression.

A nauseous unease swept over Jaye.

That could have been him. It still could be him, too, if Cash decided he wanted to show his property off a little more overtly, or if he was more of a cold-hearted bastard.

Princess had been sliced up and fucked over so many times; his face was almost a patchwork. There was nothing in the look they shared other than malice and the whistling wind of the void always trying to lure them down, down, down.

Cash's hand on Jaye's ass groped a little harder. Jaye tore his eyes away from Princess. Instead, he gave Cash a seductive, low purr of pleasure. Leaning in, Jaye whispered to his protector, "You want it? Let's go, right now."

"You gonna spread those cheeks for me?" Cash chuckled, too loudly.

So many sets of eyes, watching, and threatening men listening. Jaye felt dizzy. It seemed all conversation had stopped, but that was probably just the paranoia talking.

Dorrance wasn't on shift, though. The guards on duty weren't the friendly ones.

"Anytime, anyplace. You know me."

"Soon," Cash promised, letting go and picking up a fork instead.

The phantom tickling lasted all afternoon. Coming in from the exercise yard, Jaye hurried to the bathroom to take a leak. The constant mental pressure was manifesting in heaviness in his bladder.

Everyone else fell back. A guard accompanied Jaye and one other, elderly, prisoner to the latrines. The old man finished before Jaye, leaving him alone in the cavernous echo-chamber, his dick held in his hand. As the creepy groping slunk down between his legs, Jaye let his nerves get the best of him.

He glanced back over his shoulder for the guard as his stream of urine finally dried up.

The guard was gone.

The bathroom was as perfectly silent as a held breath before a scream.

He didn't even see it coming. He'd been looking the wrong way.

Jaye's head was pushed from behind with powerful force. The front of his skull collided with the painted cinderblock wall hard enough to make everything gray out. Instinct helped him react quickly as he managed to grab the top of the urinal when he started to collapse. Otherwise, he would have fallen face-first into the pool of his piss.

Again, his head was knocked against the unyielding wall. Ringing in his ears and fog in his head dulled his awareness.

Somewhere far away, he was moaning, slurring syllables that wouldn't string together.

The rough, cold cinderblock was flat against his face. His arms were twisted up behind his back and pinned together. Hot fluid washed down over his forehead, into his eyes, and over his lips. It tasted faintly metallic.

It felt like there was a spike lodged in the front of his head, buried deeply. Maybe it wasn't really there, but without being able to raise his arm to feel the wound, he could only judge by the pain. He knew it was impossible to survive that sort of injury, so he waited to die again, wanting to let go.

He didn't.

Instead, a wad of fabric was stuffed between his bloody lips, pushed with two fingers further back into his mouth so he couldn't spit it out. He bit down on it when something thick forced its way up his rectum. The violation was sudden and vicious enough that he could feel things tearing apart inside.

Screaming against the gag, he felt the thing inside him only push further, ripping its way deeper.

Jaye wanted to fight, but the pain had him. He was just a pig on a stick.

His feet slipped uselessly on the tile floor. Pathetic hiccups interspersed his rough, desperate yells. The agony in his straining shoulders only added to his misery as they took his full weight.

He saw nothing, only a film of red.

He heard nothing other than his own muffled, shrill shrieks and the pounding of his heart in his ears as head, ass, and shoulders fought for dominance in the losing battle for the focus of his attention.

The faster his attacker fucked him, ramming into Jaye's limp body, the more that particular pain took him over. It made him frantic. Trying to free his arms was useless. Kicking only caused him to slam his kneecaps into the cinderblock wall he was pressed against.

So, he did the only thing he could.

He gave up, went limp.

From directly behind him, right by his ear, a deep, unfamiliar voice laughed.

"You had this coming, faggot."

The words were whispered to him sweetly, accompanied by an extra hard thrust as the un-lubricated cock sheathed in him scraped with brutal friction along the inside of his body.

It went on long enough to provoke him to try screaming again, desperation for an end triumphing momentarily over exhaustion and physical trauma.

The attacker pulled out of Jaye's battered body.

Jaye crumpled to the floor hard enough to smack the underside of his jaw on the tile. His teeth clacked together, sending fresh, jagged shards ripping into his brain.

He was pulled up again by his hair.

"Tell Cash, he steals from us, we steal from him."

A fist, hard as iron, drove into Jaye's eye socket.

Everything went black — thick and complete.

Jaye surfaced, briefly, like a drowning man gulping for oxygen, his lips barely skimming the water's edge of consciousness.

He got one flash image as his left eye cracked open.

What he saw was Cash, with his fist closed up around the balls of a large black man, and that man's screams were even more earsplitting than Jaye's had been.

It was a bad, nightmarish sound, like a limb had just been ripped from its socket, strings of muscle, splinters of bone and flaps of skin connecting what had once been so vital. But it was just Cash, standing there with an awful, tight grin, and his fist firmly closed.

The dark snagged Jaye, and yanked him back down where even the ghosts couldn't reach.

Chapter 20
Recovery Process

"Are you with us, Mr. Larson?"

He squinted against the harsh light with the one eye that would open. The brightness instantly made tears prickle and he cringed, closing the eye again and turning his face slightly away.

"Easy now. We've eased up on your pain medication since the swelling is down today. Can you tell me how you're feeling?"

"B-bright," he said. "Too bright."

His tongue felt thick and dry, clumsy. His lips were cracked.

Sensing movement, followed by blessed, cooling darkness, he tried opening his eye again.

"Better?"

Things slowly started making sense. It helped him regulate his breathing, his pulse easing to a more normal speed. He realized he was in Health Services, in one of the private rooms reserved for more severely injured prisoners.

"Yeah. Thanks."

The nurse was female and in her late forties, maybe. He'd seen her once or twice before in his visits, but couldn't remember her name. Actually, he couldn't remember much of anything—like why he was there in the first place.

She crossed from the barred window, where she'd been adjusting the blinds. They were cleaner than the blinds in O'Neill's office. Reaching for his wrist, she pressed it with two fingers and glanced up at the clock on the wall, measuring his pulse.

"What's the last thing you remember, Mr. Larson?"

"I... I don't know."

"That okay. Take your time." She gave him a motherly sort of smile. "Well, the good news is, you have no major injuries, just two stitches to close the wound on your forehead, a nasty concussion and plenty of bruising. You've been ordered to bed rest for a few more days while we keep an eye on that head of yours, so you'll be with us a little longer."

"How long have I been here?"

"Two days."

She took his temperature next with a gadget she held up to his ear. He became more aware of the rest of his body. It seemed he was dressed in a hospital gown and nothing else. There was a deep-seated throbbing ache in his rectum and soreness in his shoulders, but mostly it was the hot pressure in his head that was bothering him.

When he shifted his legs, the ache in his ass flared, causing him to groan. The nurse noticed, pursing her lips and setting the thermometer aside.

"Do you remember being raped, Mr. Larson?" she asked gently, but it still made Jaye feel pinned down and scrutinized in a way that sent his panic skyrocketing.

Faggot.

You've had this coming, faggot.

He felt the ghosts come rushing in—all of the men who had ever attacked him. It was too many and too much to handle when he barely had a clue what was going on. One need became blazingly clear, fast.

"M-my meds? I need my meds. For anxiety, a-and anti-psy—"

"Okay. Okay, I'll check with the doctor, all right?" She took his hand, giving it a little squeeze. It didn't seem patronizing, and she didn't seem scared of him, just concerned. The sweetness of the gesture worked against him, though. He wasn't used to kindness. It was something he'd needed so profoundly since they'd killed him in the alley; he grasped for it, holding on to her hand holding his.

He quickly got choked up. She patted his arm.

"T-they know what he did? They got him?" he stammered, through his teary little gasps. He knew he sounded young, like he was still a kid and not an adult at all, which only added to the sense of helplessness.

"They know you were attacked," she assured him. "The prisoner who attacked you has been transferred to another facility. I'm not at liberty to say more than that, but you're going to be okay, Mr. Larson. You'll heal and we have therapists who—"

"I know," he interrupted. "I already visit the shrink regularly."

"Oh. Okay then. Let me go check with the doctor about your medication and I'll be right back, okay?"

He nodded, murmuring, "Thanks," as she left.

The biggest question Jaye had, which he knew he couldn't ask, was what had happened to Cash? The only image he was able to drag from his foggy memory was faint, almost dreamy. He had seen Cash in the bathroom. He could picture him, standing there, while Jaye had been collapsed on the floor. The mental picture was too specific to not be true... wasn't it? Or had Cash just been another ghost?

The only way to know for sure was to ask, but the last thing he wanted was to draw attention to his connections to the head of the Disciples.

The more Jaye puzzled over that vision, the more he began to suspect, with a powerful gut instinct, that it had been Smalls who had beaten and raped him. Smalls, Tio, and some of the other Warlords had been eyeing up Cash earlier in the dining hall. He had motive. He'd said so himself during the assault, that Cash had stolen something of theirs.

Robbery wasn't Cash's style. His business was founded on trust. It didn't work if the distributors of merchandise were also palming your shit when you weren't paying attention.

It didn't add up.

But Jaye knew he was the biggest asset Cash had—one that was personal; not professional, not business. Hurting Jaye only hurt Cash, not the rest of the Disciples, who merely tolerated Jaye because of his status as Cash's bitch.

The nurse walked back into his room, a tiny paper cup in hand and a smile on her face as she handed it over.

"Thanks, again," he told her, accepting the cup and staring at it instead of downing the orange pills right away. When he shook the cup, they clattered around dully.

I'm a junkie just like Mom now. Need to get my fix in order to get my head straight.

He hated it. As much as the pills numbed the anxiety which spiked his emotions and reactions so easily and unpredictably, and muffled the ever-present voices in his head, not to mention the phantom sensations he knew were only imagined... he didn't want it. He needed to figure out how to beat them on his own, not with drugs. Not like her.

"I can't leave until I see you take them," the nurse told him when he didn't seem to get the hint.

You had this coming.

Faggot.

Piggy.

You fucking worthless trash.

He saw Cora collapsed on her ratty old couch, barely dressed, too high to react.

He saw men carelessly pawing at her and her putting up with it because that was the only way she knew how to keep Jaye sheltered, fed and clothed. Each touch stole a piece of her sanity and self-worth away.

An invisible appendage caressed up Jaye's right thigh. He swatted it away.

The nurse frowned a little.

Fucked and fucked up. That's you, Johnny. That's all you are.

He opened up and tossed the pills back, dry swallowing both. Then he opened up again and stuck out his tongue to prove he'd really done it.

The empty little cup was sitting in his hand, not so very different than Cora's kit, sitting on her coffee table. They were both equally damning.

When the nurse reached for the cup, he asked her, softly, "It gets better, right?"

She gave his hand another little squeeze and looked sorry for him. Distantly, he could hear noises in other parts of Health Services, other voices, footsteps, and activity. Out there, life was carrying on. In his room, though, it felt very still and quiet, like he was stuck in place. Filling the void, the kind nurse told him, "No one stays low for long. There's always gonna be good times and bad. Hang in there, okay? You can do it."

He hoped she was right.

"I'm stronger than this. I know I am."

"Stronger than what?"

O'Neill's pencil scratched across the pad of paper sitting on the desk separating subject and scrutinizer. The fluorescent lights gave everything from the painted cement walls to the linoleum floors an ugly tinge. Jaye knew there was an entire world out there beyond the prison's confines. His sentence was nearly halfway over. Everything around him was a temporary issue. All he had to do in the meantime was survive.

That's what Cash was supposed to be for, but Hax had told Jaye as soon as he was released from medical that Cash had been sent to the hole again. Cash was out of the picture for a while, and that wasn't good for Jaye.

But Jaye's biggest concern wasn't the Warlords, or Tio. It was those little pills he was served every day in the medicine line in a paper cup. It was those voices in his head and those fingers touching him even when he knew they weren't really there. It was that damning, empty little paper cup.

Because he sensed they were something it wouldn't be so easy to leave behind once he was paroled.

"This," he growled, jabbing his temple with two fingers. "I know it's not real. I'm not stupid. I just have to figure out a way to make it stop."

"Recovery is a process, Mr. Larson," O'Neill said, peering over the rims of his thick black glasses. "It's good that you're striving to make progress, but I'd warn that realistic goals are important here. Are you not satisfied with the results of your prescriptions?"

Jaye sighed, sitting back in the metal framed chair and rubbing a hand through his hair, grabbing a handful of it on top of his head and making a fist. "It's not that. It's that I've never needed to be medicated before. My mom was—is—a junkie. *I'm* not a junkie."

"I see. There is a big difference between illegal substance abuse and appropriately, chemically treating a real psychological condition with a doctor's approval."

"Not to me." Jaye shook his head, knowing the anger was right on the surface, but without a clue as to how to bury it back down, or if he even wanted to anymore. "You say I have a condition. I don't agree. I was raped, nearly gutted, nearly murdered. And things have not exactly been easy on me in here, either. Going through hell doesn't make you sick."

"Sometimes it does," the therapist gently replied. "Consider soldiers returning from war. Some traumas are difficult to forget. Sometimes help is needed, and that's okay."

Jaye saw flashes of images, one after another, in his mind's eye — the faces of the lawyers and the judge at his trial, the faces of the doctors and nurses who treated his stab wound. They were all strangers. No one had known him. No one had really cared. The memories caused a tight feeling in the center of his chest that just twisted and twisted up even more.

"What is it, Mr. Larson?"

Jaye realized he was actually clasping his chest, feeling pinned down and wrung out.

"Maybe it all would have been easier if someone had come to see me," Jaye confessed quietly, without the courage to make eye contact with the only real person able to hear. "During my hospital stay, or when I went to the convalescent center. During the trial, or when I was locked up in Anchorage, near home. Just... *someone*, you know? No one fucking came. I'm alone. I'm all alone. I don't know if I can do this alone."

Somehow, Jaye managed to raise his gaze, only to see his therapist wearing a sort of helpless, apologetic expression that only confirmed everything Jaye already knew.

The letter arrived later that day. It was short and sweet. It was also a copy of the original, which Jaye assumed was filed away somewhere under his name in a nearby office.

His grandfather, Devon Mitchell, was dead.

The cabin Devon Mitchell had built by hand, years ago, and located way out in Bumblefuck Zus, Alaska, now belonged to Jaye, simply because he was the last living relative the estate lawyer could track down.

That sentence was the worst one.

Last living.

It was proof Jaye's mother was essentially, legally dead. Even if she was lying in a gutter somewhere, breathing and strung out, she was still dead.

Fuck, but that hurt.

Back in his cell, for a while Jaye could only lie in his bunk, numb. The letter lay folded up under his hand, every bit of it already memorized.

It was just so final.

He was locked into the cell, the upper bunk empty. Loneliness only intensified the numbness. Jaye felt a lot different than he had the last time he'd had to do without his protector. At dinner service, the Warlords had been well-represented both in the cafeteria and in the common area afterward. Jaye had passed them, not making eye contact and keeping his head held high.

Jaye knew what Cash had done. He'd ruptured Smalls' testicle like a piece of ripe, low-hanging fruit instead of a human organ, squashed with Cash's right hand until it popped.

The Warlords were enraged.

Jaye couldn't give less of a fuck. With the letter about his grandfather in his possession, the deck had been cleared. He had formal permission to write off all of humanity and care about nothing other than himself.

At least he had a place to go to. There was a shitty little cabin out there with his name on it, probably in the middle of nowhere and probably surrounded by bears or moose.

It was something, but it wasn't family or hope, and it wasn't entirely wanted.

Still, it was his.

He'd cried a little when he was alone, late at night, and it felt like whatever was left of his tattered, gutted innocence was being set on fire, burning down to ash.

There was no one now.

There was nothing.

At least I know. It's better to know than to hope like a fool.

Thinking about his predicament with the Warlords was almost a welcome indulgence compared to the reality of his practical solitude. They were a more tangible part of his life.

Since it was pretty clear he was not properly terrified, and was taking it all in stride with his thoughts on other matters, it only seemed to rile the gang more. Each time their gathered strength and nasty glares didn't anger him or get him shaking in his state-issued shoes, their expressions only became more gnarled, their collective energy blazing. Simply noticing that dynamic was remarkably empowering for Jaye. He loved being able to create such a dramatic effect while doing next to nothing. Lying on his thin, hard mattress, on top of his itchy green blanket and with the shitty letter flattened under his right hand, he quietly resolved not to take the psych meds anymore. He'd tuck them against his cheek and pull one over on the staff. No one had to know.

He needed to have his wits about him, especially since Cash was gone. He needed to keep his eyes open and his head straight. The fear had shrunk so small as to be almost inconsequential. Being afraid wasn't his problem anymore. Surviving and learning not to care about anything was all he needed to concern himself with.

Fighting back and being smart was the key. No one could fuck him up without his permission. No matter how things went down, he'd look for the narrow path through the fray, the way to dodge and weave and even play along until he could slip between the fingers of whoever wished him harm.

He was smarter than people gave him credit for. He worked as hard as he needed to and wasn't blind to the ways the world worked. Not anymore. All of the things he'd previously seen as his weaknesses — his appearance, his size, his orientation, his lack of ties to the world — were just more tools in his arsenal. The more his enemies underestimated him, the better off he was.

And Cash had given him another lesson, too. A good one. Go for the weak spots. Play dirty. Do anything it was possible to do, because the motherfuckers of the world were capable of anything. Being the one to play dirty first was a good way to get the upper hand.

Gazing up at the metal supports of Cash's bunk, Jaye said, "I'll be glad when you're back, but I plan to still be here when you do. No matter what. I can handle the assholes and the ghosts aren't real. I can do this." He let out a breath and said it again, since the only support he could count on was what came from within, not without. "I can do this."

Chapter 21
Déjà Vu

When it happened, it was quick. There was no build up of dread, and no anticipation. That was the best thing about it, making it feel like there was nothing that could have been done to avoid what went down in the exercise yard three weeks after he'd returned from his brief stay in Health Services.

A fight broke out between two guys in the Warlords' crew, over in the far corner, away from the doors. When the guards and a good majority of the other prisoners rushed over to see the punches rain down, cheering excitedly for blood and pain, Jaye hung back. He didn't need to see someone get hurt. Taking care of himself and staying out of everyone else's business was his number one priority.

But when the sea of humanity in the yard surged to the left like a tidal wave of base instincts, lapping against the chain link, barbed-wire-topped fence, someone grabbed Jaye by the shoulder. When he turned to see who it was, he twisted right onto a shiv. It was a piece of plastic snapped off in an angular blade shape, and it sunk right into the same exact spot the knife had skewered him almost a year ago.

The shock rippled outward.

There were no sounds of excited, primal yelling. There was no one around, except the man too close to see, who was several inches taller than Jaye and with brown skin. Whoever it was pulled Jaye into a close hug and jabbed the shiv a little deeper while whispering, "Shh...."

There was a bad kind of pressure in his side. As the shock wore off, the pain washed in. Jaye's mouth worked, as he tried to process the familiar, slow swell of agony spiraling outward from his abdomen. He wasn't breathing. His knees wanted to give out, so he held on to his assailant, prolonging their embrace.

Gonna twist it. Gonna twist it, Johnny. Better fight. Better man up.

He moaned. It was an abrupt sound.

He dug down deep, past the useless physical noise, to that inner reserve of strength that had allowed him to get up and run after Earl with the filleting knife instead of lying bleeding out on the asphalt. He knew it was still there. If anything, it had become easier to access.

So, his left hand grasped the base of the shiv. His right fist had a handful of his assailant's shirtfront. Grunting, shuddering, his vision graying out on the edges, he pushed his right foot forward, between the feet of the man in his arms. Then he just drew up his knee, as hard as he could, like that one action was the only thing standing between him and the reaper. Because it was.

He felt the guy's balls smash against the top of Jaye's thigh.

For a few seconds, it was messy. They struggled. The man in Jaye's arms pulled away, then pushed when Jaye wouldn't let go. Jaye fell sideways and the shiv slipped out, clattering to the concrete ground.

Crumpling to his knees, pressing with his hands against the wet, hot, seeping wound, Jaye had one glimpse of Tio's back as he jogged away, into the crowd, cupping his aching balls. Then, Tio was lost in the teeming surge and Jaye was alone again. The grey crept in farther from all sides, all directions. Blood slipped, viscous, over his fingers as he pressed harder on the gaping slice.

Tio.

It was Tio.

He's gonna pay.

The ground leapt up at him.

"Johnny!"

"Someone stuck Johnny! Hey! HEY! We need help! He needs help!"

Arms lifted him.

There was pressure on the hurt in his side, but he couldn't see a thing. It was all gray.

Tio.

Remember.

Live so you can pay him back.

Jaye didn't regain consciousness until he was out of surgery. Groggy, he opened his eyes with great effort, finding himself once more in a private Health Services room.

It was déjà vu. Same pain, but different setting.

His room was unsurprisingly empty of visitors, but this time he didn't care. That bright, light spark of hope that Kris or his mom or a friend might show up had been snuffed out completely almost a year ago. Jaye was used to the metaphorical dark now. His vision had adjusted, allowing him to see farther and clearer than he ever had before.

There was a path. He could see it.

As soon as he was able to keep his eyes open without a heaviness weighing them shut again right away, he smiled. Then, he laughed until it pulled at the stitches holding him together.

"You stupid fuckers," he croaked. The urge to laugh only grew, and it hurt, but the hurt was focused in his bad side, which only made it funnier.

It wasn't the pain meds making him loopy, although when a pretty, redheaded nurse hurried in and began to check his vitals, he was pretty sure she just thought he was stoned.

"How are you feeling, Mr. Larson?" she asked.

"You're cute," he told her, liking the shine of her copper hair. "They stabbed me, you know, right where I'd been stabbed before. Same goddamned spot."

She ignored the commentary and kept her focus on his temperature and blood pressure readings. When she lifted his sheet and bandages to examine the wound, he still couldn't stop grinning as though he'd gotten away with something.

He caught her eye as she gently pressed the tape back down to his skin, recovering his bruised, sewn-up side. "Glad you're keeping your spirits up. Seems you've been through a lot."

She was a few years older than him. Maybe she pitied him. He knew he looked younger than he was, and more fragile than he was.

"Nothing I can't handle," he said easily, letting his hand cover the vulnerable spot on his left side as she stepped back.

It felt like forever, but each day Jaye spent in Health Services was another one he could check off his sentence, and that was just fine with him.

When he was finally released and allowed to return to his cell, he kept his chin up and couldn't quite lose the grin that twisted up one side of his mouth as he made the long walk. At least he was able to not laugh outright, especially when he spied some of the Warlords eying him up.

You stupid motherfuckers.

You had a blade. You could have done anything with it, and what did you do? You did the one thing I knew right from the word go that I could come back from, no problem.

You could have sliced my throat, or gone for a major organ, and done some serious fucking damage. And what did you do instead?

Stupid motherfuckers.

Sure, he was limping a little more than he had needed to since he was first brought to Sheridan. He just let the limp add to his swagger.

At the first glimpse of his boys from the Disciples hanging out in the common area of Unit 4, Jaye's smile got out of control and he did start to laugh. Tug and Kett were all healed up, sitting at a long table with playing cards in their hands. With them were Ro, Hax, Wolf, Jinx and Gravy. Hearing Jaye's laughter, they all turned and most of them started to get to their feet.

"Johnny! Johnny's back!"

"Lookin' like a million bucks, kid! Least they coulda done was give you a damn haircut!"

"Over my dead body," someone piped up, pushing through the crowd.

"Cash!" Jaye yelled happily, feeling like a kid on Christmas morning and seeing the best, biggest gift sitting under the tree. Jogging the last few feet, he threw himself into Cash's outstretched arms which quickly and tightly embraced him. Jaye kept his left arm tucked against his bad side, but buried his face against the side of Cash's neck with a huge moan of relief. "So goddamned good to see you, boss."

Cash was clasping the back of Jaye's head, his fingers in the curls, and wrapped him with his other arm. Letting out a sigh, Cash said quietly, "Welcome back, boy. You don't know how crazy I've been missing you."

Jaye didn't want to let go, even though the guards might pry them apart at any moment. The comforting warmth and solid strength of Cash were nothing compared to the real affection he was being shown. That caring and bond were what kept Jaye going. They were worth living and fighting for.

"Felt like I was never gonna see you again," Jaye confessed.

Finally, Cash let go, stepping back slightly to get a better look. He looked as hard and grizzled as ever, but each scar, each flaw now only spoke of how skilled a survivor he was. They were his war paint, and Jaye suspected he was one of the few people in the whole world who knew who Cash really was, underneath. All of that hardness only lured Jaye in more. "How you doing? You hangin' in there?"

"No sweat," Jaye replied, smiling so big his cheeks hurt. A couple of the guys standing around clapped him on the shoulder. Zeroing in on the physical contact, Cash instantly got defensive.

"Easy, easy!" Cash warned sharply. Frowning, he moved Jaye a step or two away from the crowd and warded off any more touches.

"It's okay," Jaye laughed. "I don't break."

"I know you don't." Cash lost the frown with some effort and actually looked a little proud of his boy. He leaned in, hooking a hand behind Jaye's neck. His lips brushed Jaye's ear as he said, "We've kept hands off Tio until you got out. He's all yours if you want him."

"Hell fucking yes, I do," Jaye said eagerly. He saw Cash exchange a smirk and a nod with a few of his higher-ups.

"It's on?" Ro asked.

"Guess so," Cash answered. He stepped aside to let Jaye through and head to their shared cell. "Come on and get off your feet. You've earned it."

The guards were there but hanging back, mostly uninterested.

Eyes were on them—so many of them—but that was normal. That had been everyday life for so long; the burden of being guarded seemed more like an indulgent necessity now. Jaye knew he was play-ing a part, choosing to let his crew and the others see his happiness and lack of fear. They hadn't cowed him or put him in any sort of place he hadn't claimed for himself already. Feeling Cash's hand on his back, Jaye filled with warmth built of gratitude, pride, and readiness.

Life was good, and it was only going to get better.

Jaye had been bracing himself, thinking Cash would expect him to put out right away since they'd been apart for so long. Moving at all hurt like a bitch, and he wasn't exactly looking forward to finding out what it would feel like to have Cash's heavy body on top of him, riding him and prodding at his insides in ways he hadn't yet had to experience after either of his stabbings.

But a deal was a deal. Cash had done his part and fucked up Smalls for touching Cash's property. Now Cash had every right to partake in what belonged to him.

The lights went out. The cells were locked down. After the usual petering out of noise a few minutes later, everything was fairly still and calm.

Jaye lay there, waiting silently as the on-duty guard did a walk-by check.

The guard's darkened figure passed their doorway. As steady footsteps receded down the hall, Jaye tried to decide what to do. Pulling himself up to Cash's bunk would probably not feel too great either, but he knew he might not have a choice.

Before he could do anything, though, he saw Cash's form shifting in the darkness. The metal bed frame creaked softly. He dropped down from his bunk silently, then crawled on top of Jaye.

Mentally playing catch-up, Jaye covered his bad side with a hand to guard it from accidental pokes or nudges while Cash got the blanket over both of them. There was no moon that night and it seemed even darker than usual in the cramped little living space. Jaye could make out no details of Cash's face. He could have been anyone — bald, big, and putting out more than his share of body heat.

"Been a while," Cash murmured, slipping a hand down into Jaye's pants and palming his dick, which was still mostly soft.

"Lemme take these off," Jaye offered.

"I'll do it. Just lay there."

It wasn't Jaye's place to argue, and the attentiveness of the offer seemed to help stir Jaye's cock. Cash carefully worked Jaye's pants and boxers off, pushing them aside. Spreading his legs widely apart to let Cash settle between them, Jaye moved slowly, grimacing against each little way the muscles in his abdomen pulled. The pain was mostly imaginary. He expected it, so it manifested.

"Fuckin' hurts, don't it?"

"Not really," Jaye lied.

Cash pushed Jaye's shirt out of the way and, light as a feather, touched the wound. Jaye instinctively sucked in his stomach, shivering with dread of more pain that didn't come.

Cash's hand wrapped Jaye's cock, tugging on it.

"They think they know you. Know your weak spots. But, you know what I think?" It was making Jaye hard, the low whispering, the steady pulling on his dick when Cash had every right to only be interested in Jaye's ass and getting himself off.

Jaye shook his head and grunted.

"I think no one knows you as good as me."

The tugging got tighter, slower, and Jaye had to swallow a whimper, it was so goddamned good.

"You don't fucking move. You just lay there."

Cash had the benefit of more light to see by than Jaye, since Cash's back was to the door of their cell and some faint illumination filtered in through the narrow window in the cell's door from down the hallway. Jaye could feel Cash's scrutiny of his mouth with every little moan and quiver he made, so he played it up a little.

Cash had never done this before, trying to get Jaye off first without moving to take for himself at all, so it was a massive turn-on. And the more turned on Jaye got, the more soft sounds he made and the stiffer his dick got, sliding inside the grip of Cash's fist. Soon, his balls were drawing up. He kept expecting Cash to finger him or something, anything, and when he didn't, Jaye had to fight hard not to move. It took all of his effort to just lay there without thrusting for more, because the tugging was so slowly paced.

Shuddering, skin pebbling, nipples hard, balls aching, Jaye came with force, shooting up across his stomach and chest with a low, long moan.

Dazed and with little fireworks sizzling through the nerve endings all over his body, Jaye drew his legs up and wrapped them around Cash.

"Thought I told you not to move," Cash growled.

"Fuck me," Jaye panted. "I need your cock in me. Come on, please. I'm begging."

He could feel how hard Cash was, because the head of his dick was nudging Jaye's balls, leaving wet trails, but Cash was breathing harder, too.

"Please fuck me," Jaye pleaded in his breathy, raspy voice, letting it go soft and higher than normal.

"God damn," Cash groaned, giving Jaye two fingers, pushing them through his rim. He kissed Jaye, who gave a soft grunt at the stretch. "Tightened up, huh?"

"Cash," Jaye moaned, wanting to ride the fingers as they tugged back out, then pushed right back in, filling him up and driving him crazy. But Cash was eager. With his fingers buried, Cash spread them apart and licked into Jaye's mouth when he gasped.

"You like that?" Cash asked, sounding like he was grinning.

"Yeah," Jaye whimpered, playing it up, letting Cash feel like the big tough man dominating his little bitch. The more he felt Cash enjoying it, the more rewarding it was for Jaye. The whole thing was a thank you, after all. Cash had earned every bit of it, and more.

Cash pulled his fingers out and slicked his cock with lube without letting Jaye move much.

"Nice and easy," Cash sighed after he'd lined up and pressed to enter.

The rough cry was startled out of Jaye, because it really had been a long time. It had been months. Hurt flared from where Cash was sheathing himself in Jaye and where the shiv had pushed in, too. Holding on to Cash, hearing him hush Jaye's gasps, feeling his caress over the curve of where Jaye's ass and the top of his thigh met, Jaye opened up for it. The hurt didn't matter. All that mattered was getting every inch of Cash's thick cock buried inside and making him come so hard, he'd never forget what a good deal he had, and all of that time in the hole had been well worth it.

"Fucking hurts, don't it," Cash whispered as he bottomed out and Jaye shuddered in his arms.

Jaye's erection brushed Cash's abdomen. Jaye clenched up tightly and let his head fall back as he moaned.

"Please don't hurt me," Jaye purred.

Cash chuckled, his deep baritone vibrating through Jaye's whole body. He fed Jaye two fingers, which he sucked like they were a cock. Grinding into his ass slowly, Cash showed Jaye he intended to draw it out and make it last a long, long time. Dripping pre-come, Jaye gave little thrusts against Cash to get some relief.

"I got you, kid. No one hurts you but me. And it hurts so fucking good," Cash sighed. He pulled all the way out, gave Jaye a moment to feel empty and miss it, then sheathed himself again in one long thrust that had Jaye right on the edge of coming for a second time. The deeper Cash got, the more Jaye let go.

That's what he'd missed the most, getting to relax and trust again, just for a blessed little while.

Chapter 22
Revenge

"After breakfast. On the way out. I won't be there, but the others will."

That was as much warning as Jaye got, a few whispered words in the shower the following morning. At the time, they'd been giving the others a little show. Cash had Jaye's hair wrapped around his fist and was fucking him hard up against the wall as the shower-heads rained water down their naked bodies. Jaye was putting up more of an audible fight than a physical one, crying out like it hurt when it only felt amazing, but no one else needed to know that. Standing was much better than lying down. The position didn't press on his wound at all, so Jaye could stop worrying and just enjoy himself.

Cash pulled out, spanking Jaye's ass before turning to wash the come off his cock. Pushing his hands through his hair, blowing the water off of his lips, Jaye felt those eyes on him again, and grinned while his face was still turned against the blue-tiled wall. When he spun under the spray to face the other guys and rinse his back, he made sure to look a little less pleased with himself.

Just don't kill him, had been Cash's request that morning before they'd left the cell.

Jaye wouldn't claim to have any specific plan in mind, but he was so eager for all of the agony he was about to inflict upon that son-of-a-bitch with his shiv and payback; Jaye knew the biggest danger was letting his joy show on his face. No one could suspect, looking back on that morning, that it was Jaye dishing out some payback of his own.

But it all made sense. No one outside of the Disciples would expect Jaye to be given an active role. He was only a bitch who regularly gave up his mouth and his ass for protection. A slender, womanly teenage boy who didn't have any say in whether he got butt-fucked in the middle of a crowded prison shower or not. That was it. That tear on his face was a joke, not a warning.

Let them write me off. Let them try.

Just a pretty face and a tight ass. Something to stick knives and cocks into. Nothing more.

On his way out of the showers, proceeding along slowly in the line of guys from Unit 4, he gave Dorrance a faint smile. Dorrance gave Jaye's towel-wrapped, bare midsection a hungry, lingering glance and grinned back.

Later, when Perez handed Jaye his tray in the food line, the plate was a little unbalanced. Next to his bowl of oatmeal, orange, three slices of bread, two small cartons of milk, packets of jelly and margarine was some extra cutlery. Dorrance was the only guard nearby, and he didn't bat an eye when Jaye walked past. Once he was seated, Jaye palmed the extra spoon and tucked it inside the waistband of his pants.

Jaye didn't eat a bite of breakfast, but he kept tight hold of the spoon he'd been issued, as all prisoners were. It was an ugly brown color, made of a strange kind of plastic that was bendable and impossible to break. The spoon in his waistband was the same.

He was seated next to Cash, as usual, but didn't make eye contact with him and they didn't converse at all, though Cash was getting some of the usual types of gossip from the rest of the crew. Once in a while, Jaye stirred his serving of watery, bland oatmeal—something they were served several times a week. When he decided he was done, he got up to toss the contents of his tray. Before he stood, he quickly tucked the extra spoon up his sleeve so he'd have it closer to hand and in a more secure spot. The untouched orange was claimed by one of the elderly, non-gang-oriented inmates, whose name Jaye didn't know, by the trashcans right before Jaye could spill it over. The oatmeal, his bread, milk and condiments went in the can. The dirty tray went on the stack to be washed. His cup and spoon were returned to their place on the kitchen's shadow board, where it was easy to see at a glance if there was anything missing.

Inmates of every size, race and age were everywhere, filing out of the cafeteria, murmuring in conversation. Hax was just behind Jaye,

Ro slightly in front and on his left. Tug and Wolf were nowhere to be seen. Cash was up ahead a few steps and kept on walking when Hax guided Jaye to the right and into a storage room after Ro eased the door opened.

Hax pulled the door shut.

In the storage room, between shelves of folded linens and a tall stack of large boxes marked with types of food, like grits, soup, and beans, Wolf had Tio in a headlock. There was a dishtowel from a nearby stack stuffed in Tio's mouth. Tio was unsuccessfully trying to pry Wolf's arm off his windpipe. Tug was there, as were Kett and Gravy.

"Pin him to the floor. I just need to get at his face," Jaye told them.

He let the rest of the gang wrestle Tio to the ground and spread out his limbs, immobilizing him. Jaye slipped the extra brown spoon out of his sleeve and bit his lip, his plan coalescing at last.

"What're you thinkin', Johnny?" Ro asked. Tio was down. He struggled but wasn't moving an inch with six guys holding him. "We don't have much time here."

Softly, Jaye said, "I'm thinking he's got real pretty eyes."

They all turned to look at him, but no one said a word. On the floor, figuring it out, Tio screamed behind the gag and fought even harder. He still wasn't budging, so Jaye climbed on top of Tio's torso, straddling it while the others held his arms and legs.

It didn't take much effort at all to slip the spoon between Tio's eyelid and eyeball and twist.

From behind Jaye, one of the guys cursed and made a retching sound, but it was lost in an ear-splitting shrieking from Tio. The eye was still attached but lying on Tio's cheek. He bucked and his shrieking climbed higher and higher, especially when Jaye moved to work the bloody spoon into Tio's other eye socket. Riding Tio's writhing frantic form, Jaye bit his lip even harder, enough to draw blood, and thought of nothing but efficiently finishing the job.

When it was done, he hopped off and wiped down the spoon with another hand towel from a nearby stack, just in case they tried to take prints. The second eye hadn't come out. The spoon's edge had gored it. Blood and eye gunk was oozing over Tio's face. Everyone let him go. Tio's hands flew to his face as he thrashed around on the ground, making awful, primal sounds.

"You ready, Johnny?" Hax asked, steadying him by gripping his shoulder and cocking back an arm.

"Yeah, make it look good," Jaye replied, standing still and feeling calm.

The punch hurt in an annoying, temporary way, connecting with his left cheekbone. When Jaye crumpled to the ground, it was just part of the act.

Two guards rushed the room seconds later, finally detecting the muffled screaming. Jaye didn't see them surveying the scene; he just sensed the heavy pause before they got past their shock and could actually jump into action.

The guards called for backup. Jaye stayed curled up in a ball, clutching his eye and making terrified noises off to the side of things.

It was chaos. A gurney was brought in for Tio, whose screams were ear-splitting once they stupidly removed the towel from his mouth.

Jaye covered his ears instead until Tio was wheeled away and the noise faded a little. Then the present members of the Disciples, who'd hung around instead of trying to bolt, were handcuffed and led away toward administrative segregation while those lucky, lucky guards got to try to figure out what the hell had just happened.

Once they were each thrown into their own isolated cells, it was nothing but eerie quiet for a while. They were informally questioned by a few of the guards, but no one was talking. Some of the other inmates had seen the slow, steady procession of the Disciples through the halls. All of them had some blood splatters on them. There had been plenty for them to swipe up and stain their clothes with. The more they looked the same; the better their plan would go off.

Jaye crouched in the corner of the cot in his cell in solitary, faced with four blank walls and a heavy, solid metal door. His hands shook just a little. He knew he should wash up, but he couldn't move yet.

Tell Cash, he steals from us, we steal from him.

The Warlords had tried to kill Jaye again, the same way as before.

But they had been stupid. Jaye knew the blame didn't entirely fall on Tio. The orders had come from higher up. Tio had done it though. He'd stabbed Jaye in the same damn spot as he'd been stabbed before. Tio hadn't twisted the shiv to tear up his guts. He hadn't put it together that if Jaye had survived the injury once, he could do it again.

With that shiv, Tio could have done anything. He could have cut Jaye's throat, or sliced instead of jabbed. He could even have gouged out Jaye's eyes. But he hadn't. He'd done the one thing he shouldn't have.

You had this coming. Faggot.

Did he?

Jaye remembered the shocking, nauseating way the plastic had punched through his skin, digging into the meat of him, where it didn't belong.

At least it wasn't fingers.

Gonna slice open your belly. Pull your insides out. Make you watch.

In memory, his face smashed into the painted cement block wall. It was all in his imagination, but it hurt like it was real. He curled forward on the bed, pressing his face against the soft blanket and moaning. There was a dry, thick cock digging into his ass. There were fingers down his throat, making him need to puke.

He scrambled off the bed and lunged for the toilet, vomiting into it with enough force to leave him lightheaded.

The ghosts' voices overlapped, multiplying until there was no telling them apart.

The cell door opened. Keys jingled.

Footsteps knocked softly against the linoleum-covered cement.

Jaye clutched the metal bowl, a string of saliva trailing down from his quivering lower lip. He retched but nothing would come up.

"Let's go, Larson. Clean yourself up. Warden wants to talk to you."

They're just gonna keep coming for you, piggy. Gonna carve you up, make you squeal, fry you like bacon.

"I just want it to be over! I just want it to stop!" Jaye cried.

"Come on," the guard sighed, like they expected his ranting and didn't give a shit about it.

Jaye rinsed his hands in the small sink, splashed water on his face, too, and washed out his mouth.

The guard put the cuffs on Jaye and pushed him to walk in front.

A few minutes and a lot of limping, shuffling steps later, he was brought into a fairly nice office with carpeting, lamps, a mini-fridge and several other luxuries he'd personally long since become unaccustomed to enjoying. He was told to take the seat across from the warden, dressed in a navy blue suit and waiting with folded hands behind her imposing wooden desk. She looked perplexed more than anything.

"Tell me what happened in there with Tio Williams," she said tiredly. "The whole story."

Jaye felt tickling touches skimming up the insides of his thighs. He swatted them away and cleared his throat. The warden was frowning at him.

"They're not here, you dumb shit. They're in your head. Get it together," Jaye mumbled softly, closing his eyes and wishing the ghosts away.

"Mr. Larson? Is there a problem?"

"No. No problem." He cleared his throat again and tried to focus, sitting up straighter.

The warden glanced down at the file open in front of her. "You're taking your medication, correct? Is it not helping?"

Gonna squeal, piggy? Gonna cry?

Go on; tell the pretty lady how you plucked out his eyes. Tell her how all you are is meat. Wet, hot, and waiting for cocks and knives. Isn't that right, piggy?

"S-stress triggers it," Jaye said too loudly, talking over the ghost voices. "Been a... stressful day."

"That's understandable. But I need you to try to tell me what happened."

Jaye hummed, just trying to sit still and think in a straight line. The cement wall kept rushing up at him, and the monstrously long filleting knife kept skewering his belly, over and over again.

He leaned forward and pressed the heels of his hands to his temple. He winced at the flair of pain from his bruised eye socket.

"Tio pulled me into the storage room on the way out of the dining hall," he started, letting fear creep into his voice. "And I thought that was it, you know? He was going to finish what he started and gut me, and..." his voice wavered. He pushed invisible hands away from his stomach. "I tried to run, to push him off of me, so he punched me in the eye, kicked me to the ground. Before I could recover or get up...

I mean, my eye hurt and I was just... scared. The others. The Disciples crew. They came in. I mean, they knew it was him that stuck me before, so they pulled him away from me and... it just all happened so fast. I didn't see anything. I was a-a coward. Covered my face and cried like a bitch when I heard the s-screaming. One of the guys grabbed me, tried to pull me to my feet, but all I could see was blood a-and gore and... his fucking *eyes*... So I fought and just hid. I didn't want to be near it. I just wanted to be left alone!"

The warden was biting down hard on her back teeth. A frown line ran down the center of her brow. She tapped a pencil against the papers on her desk.

After a moment, she nodded.

"You believe he was going to attack you again?"

"It's never gonna be over. He's never gonna stop," Jaye breathed, trembling. It wasn't even part of the act. Jaye knew Tio would be joining his ghosts, ready to fuck him up all day and all night, whenever Jaye's scrambled brain decided he needed some pain.

"No, I think it will stop. Tio Williams is blind now, Mr. Larson. He won't be coming after you anymore."

Chapter 23
Rising Up

Jaye was returned to administrative segregation, along with everyone else. Their stories lined up and no one was talking, so no one was singled out as the attacker. They had no proof, and Tio wasn't talking either. Jaye knew, because Hax was in the next cell, and when Jaye yelled, "Everyone good?!"

Hax replied, "All good, Johnny!"

No one came for Jaye. No one said one word insinuating that he was the attacker. As far as the warden was concerned, Jaye was the victim, maybe more so even than Tio.

The longer Jaye lingered in solitary, safeguarded in his isolation, the more he smiled and laughed at the whole thing, moving steadily past the shock. To pass the time, he thought of that cabin he'd inherited, tucked away in the wilderness, with no one around, and no one to bother him ever again.

It was hard to tell when one day ended and another began. He slept when he was tired and exercised to keep busy, keep the ghosts away, especially since he'd been bypassing his meds for days on end. The more he worked out, the stronger he felt and the more his side continued to heal.

It was a week or two later when Ecker showed up.

The door to Jaye's cell in solitary opened and shut with a heavy bang as Ecker stepped inside, baton in hand. He smiled like he was remembering all of the ways his spindly, alien fingers had been poked deep inside Jaye's young body, over and over again. It was a serial rapist's cocky grin.

With one hand on his belt, Ecker eased closer to where Jaye was curled up on the cot in the far corner of the cell, saying, "You're gonna be really fucking sorry you landed in here, piggy. Not gonna be much of you left by the time Cash gets you back."

Ecker palmed his dick, kneading it and licking over his lips. His gaze drifted hungrily down over Jaye's body.

"Got you all to myself for the whole night. You know what I can do with a *whole night* with a little piggy like you?" He raised the baton, tilting it at the same angle his dick would be lifted to, if it was hard and swinging free. Then he pumped it and said, "You're getting a ride on this, to start with, and it's really, *really* gonna hurt—"

Heart pounding, his hope a narrow, razor-thin path through the blackness, Jaye said, soft and scary, but perfectly clearly, "Those are real pretty eyes you have."

Ecker paused.

Tio.

That's right you motherfucking piece of shit.

You heard about how Tio's eye was lying on his cheek, the other just a smear of goo and blood.

And they don't know who did it, but....

"C'mere," Jaye smiled, waving Ecker on.

There was an inner struggle happening, which Jaye could only guess at. But Ecker lost the cocky grin. The baton dropped to his side. He glanced, once, back at the door.

Ecker could press his luck, and come close enough to Jaye to poke those long fingers inside him again, but if he was close enough to do that, he was close enough for Jaye to get his hands on Ecker, too. And Jaye had motive. More than that, he might also have evidence of misconduct if someone started screaming while fingers or batons were lodged in Jaye's body.

Any way Ecker played it, if he came any closer, things would get messy.

Tio was messy too.

Jaye laughed.

Once he started, he couldn't stop. The chuckle became a full, hearty belly laugh.

Ecker turned and went back to the cell door. He unlocked it and left. Jaye was laughing so hard, tears streamed down his face and his stomach cramped up.

Slowly, he collected himself. The fit passed, and he said to himself, calm and contented, "There's no one else here."

"Hey Johnny! Looking good, kid!" Wolf called with a wink and a sly grin.

"Oh, I know," Jaye called back, tossing Wolf a wink of his own. Laughing, Wolf clapped Gravy on the back and shook his head.

Cash joined in with his own chuckles. He hooked an arm around Jaye's shoulders and asked with an intimate, low whisper against Jaye's ear, "Where the hell's that shy, pants-shitting teenager that walked in here way back when?"

"Oh, he fucking died," Jaye said seriously. "Didn't you hear? No one left but us ghosts!"

Cash's grin grew, but his gaze heated, drifting lower to lingeringly appreciate every inch of the body that belonged to him. He stroked Jaye's long curls and scanned the room. They were in the common area, sitting in rows upon rows of folding chairs tucked right up next to each other as they waited for the movie to start. Most of the lights overhead had been temporarily shut off as they gathered round the little television in anticipation of the evening's entertainment.

"Christ, but you're a kick in the pants," Cash sighed. "You know it?"

The Warlords were arranged in a cluster on the opposite side of the room, in their own chairs. Months had passed since Tio went mysteriously blind. Jaye leaned back into Cash's embrace and took a long, slow look over the faces of the rival gang.

No one made eye contact, or even got close. Jaye scanned the rest of the room. No one was staring or leering at him. Hax gave him a smile and Ro gave him a respectful nod, but that was it.

The space he'd needed like air, free of any whiff of imminent rape or murder, was finally his. It had been that way ever since the Disciples had been released from solitary. The warden had given up searching for Tio's attacker. The entire crew had paid the price with a prolonged stay in the hole, but now they were out. It was over.

Tio was there, about thirty feet away. His left eye was back in his head, but it didn't see much anymore. Covering the empty socket where his right eye should be was a black patch.

Cash hadn't gotten even a whisper of a threat from the Warlords. He'd been listening for one, but it had been calm. No one knew that Jaye had done it, but at the same time, everyone knew he'd done it. They could tell from the way the Disciples now treated Jaye with the utmost respect that he'd been initiated as a full member. The spider-web tattoo on his elbow, still healing, was the proof. Jaye wasn't just a piece of ass, and a bitch. He was a real threat. He could, and did, hold his own.

Ecker was around, but he stayed away. He no longer had the ability to scare Jaye as he did before. After being to hell and back more than once, Jaye didn't have time to worry about a jackass. Not when there were real demons, waiting in the dark.

But their teeth weren't real. They could threaten, but they would never bite, and that truth was enough to get Jaye through the rough spots. It was all in his head, after all.

A few more lights were shut off. The guards on duty gathered around behind the seated inmates. The movie started. It was The Sound of Music, and Jaye was looking forward to enjoying the greenery of the German countryside in the background.

Cash slipped a hand into Jaye's lap, kneading his dick, which started to get hard at the first graze of Cash's talented fingertips.

Jaye turned his mouth toward Cash's ear and whispered, "You know I'd suck you right now, if you wanted me to."

"I know," Cash murmured in reply. "Watch your movie. We've got time."

"But later...?"

"Later," Cash promised.

"Good. Can't wait." Jaye smiled widely and chuckled. All around him, dangerous men made sure not to catch his eye. Jaye noticed every look he didn't get, every threat that wasn't made. There was nothing he couldn't handle. Not anymore. Now the whole world was *his* bitch. And, like Cash said, it was only a matter of time....

If you enjoyed this story, you can sign up for a free membership at ForbiddenFiction and discuss it with other readers and the author at the *Caged Jaye* story page.

We do our best to proof all our work, but if you spot a text error we missed, please let us know via our website Contact Form.

Author's Notes

Going in, I knew this book was going to be one of my greatest challenges to date. I realized it was going to primarily take place inside of prison — a place I have, quite thankfully, never been. Like its predecessor, *Arctic Absolution*, this story entailed a massive amount of research before I could type a single word. Not only did I have to familiarize myself with the process of incarceration and what it means to live day in and day out inside the walls of a federal prison, but I needed to weave into every interaction the gang that becomes Jaye's adoptive family.

FCI Sheridan prison is the bones of this story, but the Disciples are the lifeblood. They keep Jaye alive and functioning from his first day inside, all the way until his last. Jaye knows his physical traits and identity make him a target. This self-awareness, as well as his willingness to do anything he has to in order to save himself, is what allows him to connect with the broader network of the Disciples. Fleshing out each member was important in bringing humanity and history to Jaye's new home. Imperfect but fearsome, these men have their own stories to tell after surviving their own initiations, and faced with varying stretches of time owed to the system. Giving them weight and mystery was one of my primary goals in this book driven, for once, not at all by romance. Though Cash is certainly Jaye's counterpart, it is the entirety of the gang and the rules of the prison that Jaye relies on with the fervency of a drowning man gasping for a dwindling pocket of blessed air.

Cash was someone I knew my readers would expect to dislike, if not hate, right from the start. My challenge, at which I hope to have succeeded, was to hint at the depths to who he really is beneath the face he presents to the Disciples, so that he could be seen not as an enemy, but as a figure firmly planted in the grey areas of the spectrum of humanity. Jaye constantly entrusts Cash with his life, with good reason. Their fates become intertwined for a brief span of years, and the influence he has on the sweet, innocent boy who entered FCI Sheridan, is profound. I might argue, though, that the opposite is just as true, and Cash would never again be the same man he was before Jaye walked with so much determination into his life.

And then there is my beautiful, broken Jaye. Every story ever written requires its hero to suffer at some point, in some way. Out of all of the dark stories I've written, Jaye's trajectory is without question the most extreme. His life after he is released from prison has already been established in *Arctic Absolution*. *Caged Jaye* is the dismantling of a fairly normal, optimistic gay teenager, taking away everything he has, including health, the guarantee of survival and his sanity. Yet by the end of the book, I feel that Jaye is the strongest character I've ever created. The thrill of explaining the ways he gets to the end and the source of the unshakable pride he finds in himself when he gets there is what enabled me to write this story as quickly as I did. After all, I knew Jaye made it out, and felt he deserved to share all of the hard-won triumphs of how he accomplished it.

Thanks must go to my editor, Rylan Hunter, who sparked the idea for this book and without whom it wouldn't exist; to my publisher, D.M. Atkins, for bringing this and all of my books to life; to T.J. Parsell, author of *Fish: A Memoir of a Boy in a Man's Prison*, for the inspiration and demonstrating that what the human spirit is capable of overcoming in the face of the cruelest, most unfair circumstances is absolutely phenomenal; to my husband and kids for their patience and love; and to my readers — I wish you all happiness.

— Lynn Kelling

About the Author

Website: www.lynnkelling.com

Lynn Kelling began writing in order to tell stories that aren't afraid of the dark, don't hold anything back and always strive to be memorable, forging lasting attachments between character and reader. Her inspiration comes from taking a closer look at behaviors and ideas lurking at the fringes of life — basically anything that people may hesitate to speak of in mixed company, but everyone wonders about anyway. Her work is driven by the taboo in order to expose the humanity within it. Lynn is an artist, designer and lover of any form of creative self-expression that comes from a place of honesty and emotion, whether it's body art or opera. She has had multiple novels published, has written over seventy works of erotic fiction of varying lengths, and always has several novels in progress.

Works by Lynn Kelling:

Deliver Us Series:
Deliver Us
From Temptation
Forgive Us

Twin Ties Series:
My Brother's Lover
Dual Affairs
Double Heat

Manse Series:
Loving the Master
Learning from the Master
Bound by Lies

Other Works:
Whatever the Cost
Song of the Lonesome Cowboy

Arctic Absolution
Caged Jaye

Threshold (Anthology)
Cursed Blessings (short story)

About the Publisher

ForbiddenFiction.com is a publisher devoted to writing that breaks the boundaries of original erotic fiction. Our stories combine intense sexuality with quality writing. Stories at Forbidden Fiction.com not only arouse readers through sensations, but also engage them emotionally and mentally through storytelling as well-crafted as the sex is hot.

ForbiddenFiction.com is also designed to be a social reading environment. You'll have fun even if just reading the latest post each day, yet you will have the chance for so much more. Readers and authors can be part of ongoing discussions of specific works and individual authors as well as more general topics.

Sign up for a FREE Membership today at ForbiddenFiction.com